CRITTENDEN

A KENTUCKY STORY OF
LOVE AND WAR

BY

JOHN FOX, JR.

ILLUSTRATED BY
F. GRAHAM COOTES

NEW YORK
CHARLES SCRIBNER'S SONS
1909

To

THE MASTER OF
BALLYHOO

ILLUSTRATIONS

CRITTENDEN

I

DAY breaking on the edge of the Bluegrass and birds singing the dawn in. Ten minutes swiftly along the sunrise and the world is changed: from nervous exaltation of atmosphere to an air of balm and peace; from grim hills to the rolling sweep of green slopes; from a high mist of thin verdure to low wind-shaken banners of young leaves; from giant poplar to white ash and sugar-tree; from log-cabin to homesteads of brick and stone; from wood-thrush to meadow-lark; rhododendron to bluegrass; from mountain to lowland, Crittenden was passing home.

He had been in the backwoods for more than a month, ostensibly to fish and look at coal lands, but, really, to get away for a while, as his custom was, from his worse self to the better self that he was when he was in the mountains —alone. As usual, he had gone in with bitterness and, as usual, he had set his face home-

ward with but half a heart for the old fight
against fate and himself that seemed destined
always to end in defeat. At dusk, he heard the
word of the outer world from the lips of an old
mountaineer at the foot of the Cumberland—
the first heard, except from his mother, for full
thirty days—and the word was—war. He
smiled incredulously at the old fellow, but, unconsciously, he pushed his horse on a little
faster up the mountain, pushed him, as the
moon rose, aslant the breast of a mighty hill
and, winding at a gallop about the last down-
ward turn of the snaky path, went at full speed
alongside the big gray wall that, above him,
rose sheer a thousand feet and, straight ahead,
broke wildly and crumbled into historic Cumberland Gap. From a little knoll he saw the
railway station in the shadow of the wall, and,
on one prong of a switch, his train panting
lazily; and, with a laugh, he pulled his horse
down to a walk and then to a dead stop—his
face grave again and uplifted. Where his eyes
rested and plain in the moonlight was a rocky
path winding upward—the old Wilderness Trail
that the Kentucky pioneers had worn with moc-
casined feet more than a century before. He
had seen it a hundred times before—moved
always; but it thrilled him now, and he rode on
slowly, looking up at it. His forefathers had

2

helped blaze that trail. On one side of that wall they had fought savage and Briton for a home and a country, and on the other side they had done it again. Later, they had fought the Mexican and in time they came to fight each other, for and against the nation they had done so much to upbuild. It was even true that a Crittenden had already given his life for the very cause that was so tardily thrilling the nation now. Thus it had always been with his people straight down the bloody national highway from Yorktown to Appomattox, and if there was war, he thought proudly, as he swung from his horse—thus it would now be with him.

If there was war? He had lain awake in his berth a long while, looking out the window and wondering. He had been born among the bleeding memories of one war. The tales of his nursery had been tales of war. And though there had been talk of war through the land for weeks before he left home, it had no more seemed possible that in his lifetime could come another war than that he should live to see any other myth of his childhood come true.

Now, it was daybreak on the edge of the Blue-grass, and, like a dark truth from a white light, three tall letters leaped from the paper in his hand—War! There was a token in the very dawn, a sword-like flame flashing upward. The man in the White House had called for willing hands by the thousands to wield it, and the Kentucky Legion, that had fought in Mexico, had split in twain to fight for the North and for the South, and had come shoulder to shoulder when the breach was closed—the Legion of his own loved State—was the first body of volunteers to reach for the hilt. Regulars were gathering from the four winds to an old Southern battlefield. Already the Legion was on its way to camp in the Bluegrass. His town was making ready to welcome it, and among the names of the speakers who were to voice the welcome, he saw his own—Clay Crittenden.

II

THE train slackened speed and stopped. There was his horse—Raincrow—and his buggy waiting for him when he stepped from the platform; and, as he went forward with his fishing tackle, a livery-stable boy sprang out of the buggy and went to the horse's head.

"Bob lef' yo' hoss in town las' night, Mistuh Crittenden," he said. "Miss Rachel said yestiddy she jes knowed you was comin' home this mornin'."

Crittenden smiled—it was one of his mother's premonitions; she seemed always to know when he was coming home.

"Come get these things," he said, and went on with his paper.

"Yessuh!"

Things had gone swiftly while he was in the hills. Old ex-Confederates were answering the call from the Capitol. One of his father's old comrades—little Jerry Carter—was to be made a major-general. Among the regulars mobilizing at Chickamauga was the regiment to which Rivers, a friend of his boyhood, belonged. There,

three days later, his State was going to dedicate
two monuments to her sons who had fallen on
the old battle-field, where his father, fighting
with one wing of the Legion for the Lost Cause,
and his father's young brother, fighting with the
other against it, had fought face to face; where
his uncle met death on the field and his father
got the wound that brought death to him year:
after the war. And then he saw something that
for a moment quite blotted the war from his
brain and made him close the paper quickly.
Judith had come home—Judith was to unveil
those statues—Judith Page.

The town was asleep, except for the rattle of
milk-carts, the banging of shutters, and the
hum of a street-car, and Crittenden moved
through empty streets to the broad smooth turnpike on the south, where Raincrow shook his
head, settled his haunches, and broke into the
swinging trot peculiar to his breed—for home.

Spring in the Bluegrass! The earth spiritual
as it never is except under new-fallen snow—in
the first shy green. The leaves, a floating mist
of green, so buoyant that, if loosed, they must,
it seemed, have floated upward—never to know
the blight of frost or the droop of age. The
air, rich with the smell of new earth and sprout-
ing grass, the long, low skies newly washed and,
through radiant distances, clouds light as thistle-

6

down and white as snow. And the birds! Wrens in the hedges, sparrows by the wayside and on fence-rails, starlings poised over meadows brilliant with glistening dew, larks in the pastures—all singing as they sang at the first dawn, and the mood of nature that perfect blending of earth and heaven that is given her children but rarely to know. It was good to be alive at the breaking of such a day—good to be young and strong, and eager and unafraid, when the nation called for its young men and red Mars was the morning star. The blood of dead fighters began to leap again in his veins. His nostrils dilated and his chin was raised proudly—a racial chord touched within him that had been dumb a long while. And that was all it was—the blood of his fathers; for it was honor and not love that bound him to his own flag. He was his mother's son, and the unspoken bitterness that lurked in her heart lurked, likewise, on her account, in his.

On the top of a low hill, a wind from the dawn struck him, and the paper in the bottom of the buggy began to snap against the dashboard. He reached down to keep it from being whisked into the road, and he saw again that Judith Page had come home. When he sat up again, his face was quite changed. His head fell a little forward, his shoulders drooped

7

slightly and, for a moment, his buoyancy was gone. The corners of the mouth showed a settled melancholy where before was sunny humour. The eyes, which were dreamy, kindly, gray, looked backward in a morbid glow of concentration; and over the rather reckless cast of his features, lay at once the shadow of suffering and the light of a great tenderness. Slowly, a little hardness came into his eyes and a little bitterness about his mouth. His upper lip curved in upon his teeth with self-scorn—for he had had little cause to be pleased with himself while Judith was gone, and his eyes showed now how proud was the scorn—and he shook himself sharply and sat upright. He had forgotten again. That part of his life belonged to the past and, like the past, was gone, and was not to come back again. The present had life and hope now, and the purpose born that day from five blank years was like the sudden birth of a flower in a desert.

The sun had burst from the horizon now and was shining through the tops of the trees in the lovely woodland into which Crittenden turned, and through which a road of brown creek-sand ran to the pasture beyond and through that to the long avenue of locusts, up which the noble portico of his old homestead, Canewood, was visible among cedars and firs and old forest-trees. His mother was not up yet—the shutters of her window were still closed—but the servants were astir and busy. He could see men and plough-horses on their way to the fields; and, that far away, he could hear the sound of old Ephraim's axe at the woodpile, the noises around the barn and cowpens, and old Aunt Keziah singing a hymn in the kitchen, the old wailing cry of the mother-slave.

> "Oh I wonder whur my baby's done gone,
>   Oh Lawd!
>   An' I git on my knees an' pray."

The song stopped, a negro boy sprang out the kitchen-door and ran for the stiles—a tall, strong, and very black boy with a dancing eye, white teeth, and a look of welcome that was little short of dumb idolatry.

"Howdy, Bob."

"Howdy, Ole Cap'n." Crittenden had been "Ole Captain" with the servants—since the death of "Ole Master," his father—to distinguish him from "Young Captain," who was his brother, Basil. Master and servant shook hands and Bob's teeth flashed.

"What's the matter, Bob?"

Bob climbed into the buggy.

"You gwine to de wah."

Crittenden laughed.

9

"How do you know, Bob?"

"Oh, I know—I know. I seed it when you was drivin' up to de stiles, an' lemme tell you, Ole Cap'n." The horse started for the barn suddenly and Bob took a wide circuit in order to catch the eye of a brown milkmaid in the cowpens, who sniffed the air scornfully, to show that she did not see him, and buried the waves of her black hair into the silken sides of a young Jersey.

"Yes," he said, shaking his head and making threats to himself, "an' Bob's gwine wid him."

As Crittenden climbed the stiles, old Keziah filled the kitchen-door.

"Time you gittin' back, suh," she cried with mock severity. "I been studyin' 'bout you. Little mo' an' I'd 'a' been comin' fer you myself. Yes—suh."

And she gave a loud laugh that rang through the yard and ended in a soft, queer little whoop that was musical. Crittenden smiled but, instead of answering, raised his hand warningly and, as he approached the portico, he stepped from the gravel-walk to the thick turf and began to tiptoe. At the foot of the low flight of stone steps he stopped—smiling.

The big double front door was wide open, and straight through the big, wide hallway and at the entrance of the dining-room, a sword—a long cavalry sabre—hung with a jaunty gray cap on the wall. Under them stood a boy with his hands clasped behind him and his chin up-raised. The lad could see the bullet-hole through the top, and he knew that on the visor was a faded stain of his father's blood. As a child, he had been told never to touch the cap or sword and, until this moment, he had not wanted to take them down since he was a child; and even now the habit of obedience held him back for a while, as he stood looking up at them. Outside, a light wind rustled the leaves of the rose-bush at his mother's window, swept through the open door, and made the curtain at his el-bow swell gently. As the heavy fold fell back to its place and swung out again, it caught the hilt of the sword and made the metal point of the scabbard clank softly against the wall. The boy breathed sharply, remembered that he was grown, and reverently reached upward. There was the stain where the blood had run down from the furrowed wound that had caused his father's death, long after the war and just be-fore the boy was born. The hilt was tarnished, and when he caught it and pulled, the blade came out a little way and stuck fast. Some one stepped on the porch outside and he turned quickly, as he might have turned had some one caught him unsheathing the weapon when a child.

"Hold on there, little brother."

Crittenden stopped in the doorway, smiling affectionately, and the boy thrust the blade back to the hilt.

"Why, Clay," he cried, and, as he ran forward, "Are you going?" he asked, eagerly.

"I'm the first-born, you know," added Crittenden, still smiling, and the lad stretched the sabre out to him, repeating eagerly, "Are you going?"

The older brother did not answer, but turned, without taking the weapon, and walked to the door and back again.

"Are you?"

"Me? Oh, I have to go," said the boy solemnly and with great dignity, as though the matter were quite beyond the pale of discussion.

"You do?"

"Yes; the Legion is going."

"Only the members who volunteer—nobody has to go."

"Don't they?" said the lad, indignantly. "Well, if I had a son who belonged to a military organization in time of peace"—the lad spoke glibly—"and refused to go with it to war—well, I'd rather see him dead first."

"Who said that?" asked the otner, and the lad coloured.

"Why, Judge Page said it; that's who. And you just ought to hear Miss Judith!"

Again the other walked to the door and back again. Then he took the scabbard and drew the blade to its point as easily as though it had been oiled, thrust it back, and hung it with the cap in its place on the wall.

"Perhaps neither of us will need it," he said. "We'll both be privates—that is, if I go—and I tell you what we'll do. We'll let the better man win the sword, and the better man shall have it after the war. What do you say?"

"Say?" cried the boy, and he gave the other a hug and both started for the porch. As they passed the door of his mother's room, the lad put one finger on his lips; but the mother had heard and, inside, a woman in black, who had been standing before a mirror with her hands to her throat, let them fall suddenly until they were clasped for an instant across her breast. But she gave no sign that she had heard, at breakfast an hour later, even when the boy cleared his throat, and after many futile efforts to bring the matter up, signalled across the table to his brother for help.

"Mother, Basil there wants to go to war. He says if he had a son who belonged to a military organization in time of peace and refused to go with it in time of war, that he'd rather see him dead."

The mother's lip quivered when she answered,

but so imperceptibly that only the older son saw it.

"That is what his father would have said," she said, quietly, and Crittenden knew she had already fought out the battle with herself—alone. For a moment the boy was stunned with his good fortune—"it was too easy"—and with a whoop he sprang from his place and caught his mother around the neck, while Uncle Ben, the black butler, shook his head and hurried into the kitchen for corn-bread and to tell the news.

"Oh, I tell you it's great fun to *have* to go to war! Mother," added the boy, with quick mischief, "Clay wants to go, too."

Crittenden braced himself and looked up with one quick glance sidewise at his mother's face. It had not changed a line.

"I heard all you said in the hallway. If a son of mine thinks it his duty to go, I shall never say one word to dissuade him—if he thinks it is his duty," she added, so solemnly that silence fell upon the three, and with a smothered, "Good Lawd," at the door, Ben hurried again into the kitchen.

"Both them boys was a-goin' off to git killed an' ole Miss Rachel not sayin' one wud to keep 'em back—not a wud."

After breakfast the boy hurried out and, as

Crittenden rose, the mother, who pretended to be arranging silver at the old sideboard, spoke with her back to him.

"Think it over, son. I can't see that you should go, but if you think you ought, I shall have nothing to say. Have you made up your mind?"

Crittenden hesitated.

"Not quite."

"Think it over very carefully, then—please—for my sake." Her voice trembled, and, with a pang, Crittenden thought of the suffering she had known from one war. Basil's way was clear, and he could never ask the boy to give up to him because he was the elder. Was it fair to his brave mother for him to go, too—was it right?

"Yes, mother," he said, soberly.

III

THE Legion came next morning and pitched camp in a woodland of oak and sugar trees, where was to be voiced a patriotic welcome by a great editor, a great orator, and young Crittenden.

Before noon, company streets were laid out and lined with tents and, when the first buggies and rockaways began to roll in from the country, every boy-soldier was brushed and burnished to defy the stare of inspection and to quite dazzle the eye of masculine envy or feminine admiration.

In the centre of the woodland was a big auditorium, where the speaking was to take place. After the orators were done, there was to be a regimental review in the bluegrass pasture in front of historic Ashland. It was at the Colonel's tent, where Crittenden went to pay his respects, that he found Judith Page, and he stopped for a moment under an oak, taking in the gay party of women and officers who sat and stood about the entrance. In the centre of the group stood a lieutenant in the blue of a regular and with the crossed sabres of the cavalryman on his neck-band and the number of his regiment. The girl was talking to the gallant old Colonel with her back to Crittenden, but he would have known her had he seen but an arm, a shoulder, the poise of her head, a single gesture—although he had not seen her for years. The figure was the same—a little fuller, perhaps, but graceful, round, and slender, as was the throat. The hair was a trifle darker, he thought, but brown still, and as rich with gold as autumn sunlight. The profile was in outline now—it was more cleanly cut than ever. The face was a little older, but still remarkably girlish in spite of its maturer strength; and as she turned to answer his look, he kept on unconsciously reaffirming to his memory the broad brow and deep clear eyes, even while his hand was reaching for the brim of his hat. She showed only gracious surprise at seeing him and, to his wonder, he was as calm and cool as though he were welcoming back home any good friend who had been away a long time. He could now see that the lieutenant belonged to the Tenth United States Cavalry; he knew that the Tenth was a colored regiment; he understood a certain stiffness that he felt rather than saw in the courtesy that was so carefully shown him by the Southern volunteers who were about him; and he turned away to avoid meeting him. For the same reason, he fancied, Judith turned, too. The mere idea of negro soldiers was not only repugnant to him, but he did not believe in negro regiments. These would be the men who could and would organize and drill the blacks in the South; who, in other words, would make possible, hasten, and prolong the race war that sometimes struck him as inevitable. As he turned, he saw a tall, fine-looking negro, fifty yards away, in the uniform of a sergeant of cavalry and surrounded by a crowd of gaping darkies whom he was haranguing earnestly. Lieutenant and sergeant were evidently on an enlisting tour.

Just then, a radiant little creature looked up into Crittenden's face, calling him by name and holding out both hands—Phyllis, Basil's little sweetheart. With her was a tall, keen-featured fellow, whom she introduced as a war correspondent and a Northerner.

"A sort of war correspondent," corrected Grafton, with a swift look of interest at Crittenden, but turning his eyes at once back to Phyllis. She was a new and diverting type to the Northern man and her name was fitting and pleased him. A company passed just then, and a smothered exclamation from Phyllis turned attention to it. On the end of the line, with his

18

chin in, his shoulders squared and his eyes straight forward, was Crittenden's warrior-brother, Basil. Only his face coloured to show that he knew where he was and who was looking at him, but not so much as a glance of his eye did he send toward the tent. Judith turned to Crittenden quickly:

"Your little brother is going to the war?" The question was thoughtless and significant, for it betrayed to him what was going on in her mind, and she knew it and coloured, as he paled a little.

"My little brother is going to the war," he repeated, looking at her. Judith smiled and went on bravely:

"And you?"

Crittenden, too, smiled.

"I may consider it my duty to stay at home."

The girl looked rather surprised—instead of showing the subdued sarcasm that he was looking for—and, in truth, she was. His evasive and careless answer showed an indifference to her wish and opinion in the matter that would once have been very unusual. Straightway there was a tug at her heart-strings that also was unusual.

The people were gathering into the open-air auditorium now and, from all over the camp, the crowd began to move that way. All knew the word of the orator's mouth and the word of the editor—they had heard the one and seen the other on his printed page many times; and it was for this reason, perhaps, that Crittenden's fresh fire thrilled and swayed the crowd as it did.

When he rose, he saw his mother almost under him and, not far behind her, Judith with her father, Judge Page. The lieutenant of regulars was standing on the edge of the crowd, and to his right was Grafton, also standing, with his hat under his arm—idly curious. But it was to his mother that he spoke and, steadfastly, he saw her strong, gentle face even when he was looking far over her head, and he knew that she knew that he was arguing the point then and there between them.

It was, he said, the first war of its kind in history. It marked an epoch in the growth of national character since the world began. As an American, he believed that no finger of mediævalism should so much as touch this hemisphere. The Cubans had earned their freedom long since, and the cries of starving women and children for the bread which fathers and brothers asked but the right to earn must cease. To put out of mind the Americans blown to death at Havana—if such a thing were possible—he yet believed with all his heart in the war. He did not think there would be much of a fight—the regular army could doubtless take good care of the Spaniard—but if everybody acted on that presumption, there would be no answer to the call for volunteers. He was proud to think that the Legion of his own State, that in itself stood for the reunion of the North and the South, had been the first to spring to arms. And he was proud to think that not even they were the first Kentuckians to fight for Cuban liberty. He was proud that, before the Civil War even, a Kentuckian of his own name and blood had led a band of one hundred and fifty brave men of his own State against Spanish tyranny in Cuba, and a Crittenden, with fifty of his followers, were captured and shot in platoons of six.

"A Kentuckian kneels only to woman and his God," this Crittenden had said proudly when ordered to kneel blindfolded and with his face to the wall, "and always dies facing his enemy." And so those Kentuckians had died nearly half a century before, and he knew that the young Kentuckians before him would as bravely die, if need be, in the same cause now; and when they came face to face with the Spaniard they would remember the shattered battle-ship in the Havana harbour, and something more—they would re-member Crittenden. And then the speaker closed with the words of a certain proud old Confederate soldier to his son:

"No matter who was right and who was wrong in the Civil War, the matter is settled now by the sword. The Constitution left the question open, but it is written there now in letters of blood. We have given our word that they shall stand; and remember it is the word of gentlemen and binding on their sons. There have been those in the North who have doubted that word; there have been those in the South who have given cause for doubt; and this may be true for a long time. But if ever the time comes to test that word, do you be the first to prove it. You will fight for your flag—mine now as well as yours—just as sincerely as I fought against it." And these words, said Crittenden in a trembling voice, the brave gentleman spoke again on his death-bed; and now, as he looked around on the fearless young faces about him, he had no need to fear that they were spoken in vain.

And so the time was come for the South to prove its loyalty—not to itself nor to the North, but to the world.

Under him he saw his mother's eyes fill with tears, for these words of her son were the dying words of her lion-hearted husband. And Judith had sat motionless, watching him with peculiar intensity and flushing a little, perhaps at the memory of her jesting taunt, while Grafton had stood still—his eyes fixed, his face earnest— missing not a word.   He was waiting for Crittenden, and he held his hand out when the latter emerged from the crowd, with the curious embarrassment that assails the newspaper man when he finds himself betrayed into unusual feeling.

"I say," he said; "that was good, *good!*"

The officer who, too, had stood still as a statue, seemed to be moving toward him, and again Crittenden turned away—to look for his mother. She had gone home at once—she could not face him now in that crowd—and as he was turning to his own buggy, he saw Judith and from habit started toward her, but, changing his mind, he raised his hat and kept on his way, while the memory of the girl's face kept pace with him.

She was looking at him with a curious wistfulness that was quite beyond him to interpret— a wistfulness that was in the sudden smile of welcome when she saw him start toward her and in the startled flush of surprise when he stopped; then, with the tail of his eye, he saw the quick paleness that followed as the girl's sensitive nostrils quivered once and her spirited face settled quickly into a proud calm.   And then he saw her smile—a strange little smile that may have been at herself or at him—and he wondered about it all and was tempted to go back, but kept on doggedly, wondering at her and at himself with a miserable grim satisfaction that he was at last over and above it all. She had told him to conquer his boyish love for her and, as her will had always been law to him, he had made it, at last, a law in this. The touch of the loadstone that never in his life had failed, had failed now, and now, for once in his life, desire and duty were one.

He found his mother at her seat by her open window, the unopened buds of her favourite roses hanging motionless in the still air outside, but giving their fresh green faint fragrance to the whole room within; and he remembered the quiet sunset scene every night for many nights to come. Every line in her patient face had been traced there by a sorrow of the old war, and his voice trembled:

"Mother," he said, as he bent down and kissed her, "I'm going."

Her head dropped quickly to the work in her lap, but she said nothing, and he went quickly out again.

IV

IT was growing dusk outside. Chickens were
going to roost with a great chattering in
some locust-trees in one corner of the yard. An
aged darkey was swinging an axe at the wood-
pile and two little pickaninnies were gathering a
basket of chips. Already the air was filled with
the twilight sounds of the farm—the lowing of
cattle, the bleating of calves at the cowpens, the
bleat of sheep from the woods, and the nicker
of horses in the barn. Through it all, Crittenden could hear the nervous thud of Raincrow's
hoofs announcing rain—for that was the way
the horse got his name, being as black as a
crow and, as Bob claimed, always knowing
when falling weather was at hand and speaking
his prophecy by stamping in his stall. He could
hear Basil noisily making his way to the barn.
As he walked through the garden toward the
old family graveyard, he could still hear the boy,
and a prescient tithe of the pain, that he felt
would strike him in full some day, smote him so
sharply now that he stopped a moment to listen,
with one hand quickly raised to his forehead.
Basil was whistling—whistling joyously. Fore-

boding touched the boy like the brush of a bird's wing, and death and sorrow were as remote as infinity to him. At the barn-door the lad called sharply:

"Bob!"

"Suh!" answered a muffled voice, and Bob emerged, gray with oatdust.

"I want my buggy to-night." Bob grinned.

"Sidebar?"

"Yes."

"New whip—new harness—little buggy mare —reckon?"

"I want 'em all."

Bob laughed loudly. "Oh, I know. You gwine to see Miss Phyllis dis night, sho—yes, Lawd!" Bob dodged a kick from the toe of the boy's boot—a playful kick that was not meant to land—and went into the barn and came out again.

"Yes, an' I know somewhur else you gwine— you gwine to de war. Oh, I know; yes, suh. Dere's a white man in town tryin' to git niggers to 'list wid him, an' he's got a nigger sojer what say he's a officer hisself; yes, mon, a corpril. An' dis nigger's jes a-gwine through town drawin' niggers right *an'* left. He talk to me, but I jes laugh at him, an' say I gwine wid Ole Cap'n ur Young Cap'n, I don't keer which. An' lemme tell you, Young Capn', ef you ur

26

Ole Cap'n doan lemme go wid you, I'se gwine wid dat nigger corpril an' dat white man what 'long to a nigger regiment, an' I know you don't want me to bring no sech disgrace on de fambly dat way—no, suh. He axe what you de cap'n of," Bob went on, aiming at two birds with one stone now, "an' I say you de cap'n of ever'body an' ever'ting dat come 'long—dat's what I say— an' he be cap'n of you wid all yo' unyform and sich, I say, if you jest come out to de fahm—yes, mon, dat he will sho."

The boy laughed and Bob reiterated:

"Oh, I'se gwine—I'se gwine wid you—" Then he stopped short. The turbaned figure of Aunt Keziah loomed from behind the wood-pile.

"What dat I heah 'bout you gwine to de wah, nigger, what dat I heah?"

Bob laughed—but it was a laugh of propitiation.

"Law, mammy. I was jes projeckin' wid Young Cap'n."

"Fool nigger, doan know what wah is—doan lemme heah you talk no more 'bout gwine to de wah ur I gwine to w'ar you out wid a hickory— dat's whut I'll do—now you min'." She turned on Basil then; but Basil had retreated, and his laugh rang from the darkening yard. She cried after him:

"An' doan lemme heah you puttin' dis fool

nigger up to gittin' hisself killed by dem Cubians neither; no suh!" She was deadly serious now. "I done spanked you heap o' times, an' 'tain't so long ago, an' you ain' too big yit; no, suh." The old woman's wrath was rising higher, and Bob darted into the barn before she could turn back again to him, and a moment later darted his head, like a woodpecker, out again to see if she were gone, and grinned silently after her as she rolled angrily toward the house, scolding both Bob and Basil to herself loudly.

A song rose from the cowpens just then. Full, clear, and quivering, it seemed suddenly to still everything else into silence. In a flash, Bob's grin settled into a look of sullen dejection, and, with his ear cocked and drinking in the song, and with his eye on the corner of the barn, he waited. From the cowpens was coming a sturdy negro girl with a bucket of foaming milk in each hand and a third balanced on her head, singing with all the strength of her lungs. In a moment she passed the corner.

"Molly—say, Molly."

The song stopped short.

"Say, honey, wait a minute—jes a minute, won't ye?" The milkmaid kept straight ahead, and Bob's honeyed words soured suddenly.

"Go on, gal, think yo'self mighty fine, don't ye? Nem' min'!"

28

Molly's nostrils swelled to their full width, and, at the top of her voice, she began again.

"Go on, nigger, but you jes wait."

Molly sang on:

"Take up yo' cross, oh, sinner-man."

Before he knew it, Bob gave the response with great unction:

"Yes, Lawd."

Then he stopped short.

"I reckon I got to break dat gal's head some day. Yessuh; she knows whut my cross is," and then he started slowly after her, shaking his head and, as his wont was, talking to himself.

He was still talking to himself when Basil came out to the stiles after supper to get into his buggy.

"Young Cap'n, dat gal Molly mighty nigh pesterin' de life out o' me. I done tol' her I'se gwine to de wah."

"What did she say?"

"De fool nigger—she jes laughed—she jes laughed."

The boy, too, laughed, as he gathered the reins and the mare sprang forward.

"We'll see—we'll see."

And Bob with a triumphant snort turned toward Molly's cabin.

The locust-trees were quiet now and the barn

was still except for the occasional stamp of a horse in his stall or the squeak of a pig that was pushed out of his warm place by a stronger brother. The night noises were strong and clear—the cricket in the grass, the croaking frogs from the pool, the whir of a night-hawk's wings along the edge of the yard, the persistent wail of a whip-poor-will sitting lengthwise of a willow limb over the meadow-branch, the occasional sleepy caw of crows from their roost in the woods beyond, the bark of a house-dog at a neighbour's home across the fields, and, further still, the fine high yell of a fox-hunter and the faint answering yelp of a hound.

And inside, in the mother's room, the curtain was rising on a tragedy that was tearing open the wounds of that other war—the tragedy upon which a bloody curtain had fallen more than thirty years before. The mother listened quietly, as had her mother before her, while the son spoke quietly, for time and again he had gone over the ground to himself, ending ever with the same unalterable resolve.

There had been a Crittenden in every war of the nation—down to the two Crittendens who slept side by side in the old graveyard below the garden.

And the Crittenden—of whom he had spoken that morning—the gallant Crittenden who led

his Kentuckians to death in Cuba, in 1851, was
his father's elder brother. And again he repeated the dying old Confederate's deathless
words with which he had thrilled the Legion
that morning—words heard by her own ears as
well as his. What else was left him to do—
when he knew what those three brothers, if they
were alive, would have him do ?

And there were other untold reasons, hid in
the core of his own heart, faced only when he
was alone, and faced again, that night, after he
had left his mother and was in his own room
and looking out at the moonlight and the big
weeping willow that drooped over the one white
tomb under which the two brothers, who had
been enemies in the battle, slept side by side
thus in peace. So far he had followed in their
footsteps, since the one part that he was fitted
to play was the *rôle* they and their ancestors had
played beyond the time when the first American
among them, failing to rescue his king from
Carisbrooke Castle, set sail for Virginia on the
very day Charles lost his royal head. But for
the Civil War, Crittenden would have played
that *rôle* worthily and without question to the
end. With the close of the war, however, his
birthright was gone—even before he was born—
and yet, as he grew to manhood, he had gone on
in the serene and lofty way of his father—there

was nothing else he could do—playing the gentleman still, though with each year the audience grew more restless and the other and lesser actors in the drama of Southern reconstruction more and more resented the particular claims of the star. At last, came with a shock the realization that with the passing of the war his occupation had forever gone. And all at once, out on his ancestral farm that had carried its name Canewood down from pioneer days; that had never been owned by a white man who was not a Crittenden; that was isolated, and had its slaves and the children of those slaves still as servants; that still clung rigidly to old traditions —social, agricultural, and patriarchal—out there Crittenden found himself one day alone. His friends—even the boy, his brother—had caught the modern trend of things quicker than he, and most of them had gone to work—some to law, some as clerks, railroad men, merchants, civil engineers; some to mining and speculating in the State's own rich mountains. Of course, he had studied law—his type of Southerner always studies law—and he tried the practice of it. He had too much self-confidence, perhaps, based on his own brilliant record as a college orator, and he never got over the humiliation of losing his first case, being handled like putty by a small, black-eyed youth of his own age, who had come from nowhere and had passed up through a philanthropical old judge's office to the dignity, by and by, of a license of his own. Losing the suit, through some absurd little technical mistake, Crittenden not only declined a fee, but paid the judgment against his client out of his own pocket and went home with a wound to his foolish, sensitive pride for which there was no quick cure. A little later, he went to the mountains, when those wonderful hills first began to give up their wealth to the world; but the pace was too swift, competition was too undignified and greedy, and business was won on too low a plane. After a year or two of rough life, which helped him more than he knew, until long afterward, he went home. Politics he had not yet tried, and politics he was now persuaded to try. He made a brilliant canvass, but another element than oratory had crept in as a new factor in political success. His opponent, Wharton, the wretched little lawyer who had bested him once before, bested him now, and the weight of the last straw fell crushingly. It was no use. The little touch of magic that makes success seemed to have been denied him at birth, and, therefore, deterioration began to set in—the deterioration that comes from idleness, from energy that gets the wrong vent, from strong passions that a definite purpose would have

33

kept under control—and the worse elements of
a nature that, at the bottom, was true and fine,
slowly began to take possession of him as weeds
will take possession of an abandoned field.

But even then nobody took him as seriously
as he took himself. So that while he fell just
short, in his own eyes, of everything that was
worth while; of doing something and being
something worth while; believing something
that made the next world worth while; or gain-
ing the love of a woman that would have made
this life worth while—in the eyes of his own
people he was merely sowing his wild oats after
the fashion of his race, and would settle down,
after the same fashion, by and by—that was the
indulgent summary of his career thus far.
He had been a brilliant student in the old uni-
versity and, in a desultory way, he was yet. He
had worried his professor of metaphysics by
puzzling questions and keen argument until that
philosopher was glad to mark him highest in his
class and let him go. He surprised the old
lawyers when it came to a discussion of the
pure theory of law, and, on the one occasion
when his mother's pastor came to see him, he
disturbed that good man no little, and closed
his lips against further censure of him in pulpit
or in private. So that all that was said against
him by the pious was that he did not go to

church as he should; and by the thoughtful, that he was making a shameful waste of the talents that the Almighty had showered so freely down upon him. And so without suffering greatly in public estimation, in spite of the fact that the ideals of Southern life were changing fast, he passed into the old-young period that is the critical time in the lives of men like him—when he thought he had drunk his cup to the dregs; had run the gamut of human experience; that nothing was left to his future but the dull repetition of his past. Only those who knew him best had not given up hope of him, nor had he really given up hope of himself as fully as he thought. The truth was, he never fell far, nor for long, and he always rose with the old purpose the same, even if it stirred him each time with less and less enthusiasm—and always with the beacon-light of one star shining from his past, even though each time it shone a little more dimly. For usually, of course, there is the hand of a woman on the lever that prizes such a man's life upward, and when Judith Page's clasp loosened on Crittenden, the castle that the lightest touch of her finger raised in his imagination—that he, doubtless, would have reared for her and for him, in fact, fell in quite hopeless ruins, and no similar shape was ever framed for him above its ashes.

It was the simplest and oldest of stories between the two—a story that began, doubtless, with the beginning, and will never end as long as two men and one woman, or two women and one man are left on earth—the story of the love of one who loves another.   Only, to the sufferers the tragedy is always as fresh as a knife-cut, and forever new.

Judith cared for nobody.   Crittenden laughed and pleaded, stormed, sulked, and upbraided, and was devoted and indifferent for years—like the wilful, passionate youngster that he was—until Judith did love another—what other, Crittenden never knew.   And then he really believed that he must, as she had told him so often, conquer his love for her.   And he did, at a fearful cost to the best that was in him—foolishly, but consciously, deliberately.   When the reaction came, he tried to reëstablish his relations to a world that held no Judith Page.   Her absence gave him help, and he had done very well, in spite of an occasional relapse.   It was a relapse that had sent him to the mountains, six weeks before, and he had emerged with a clear eye, a clear head, steady nerves, and with the one thing that he had always lacked, waiting for him—a purpose.   It was little wonder, then, that the first ruddy flash across a sky that had been sunny with peace for thirty years and more

thrilled him like an electric charge from the
very clouds. The next best thing to a noble life
was a death that was noble, and that was possible to any man in war. One war had taken
away—another might give back again; and his
chance was come at last.

It was midnight now, and far across the fields
came the swift faint beat of a horse's hoofs on
the turnpike. A moment later he could hear
the hum of wheels—it was his little brother
coming home; nobody had a horse that could
go like that, and nobody else would drive that
way if he had. Since the death of their father,
thirteen years after the war, he had been father
to the boy, and time and again he had wondered
now why he could not have been like that
youngster. Life was an open book to the boy
—to be read as he ran. He took it as he took
his daily bread, without thought, without question. If left alone, he and the little girl whom
he had gone that night to see would marry,
settle down, and go hand in hand into old age
without questioning love, life, or happiness.
And that was as it should be; and would to
Heaven he had been born to tread the self-same
way. There was a day when he was near it;
when he turned the same fresh, frank face fearlessly to the world, when his nature was as un-
spoiled and as clean, his hopes as high, and his

faith as child-like; and once when he ran across
a passage in Stevenson in which that gentle student spoke of his earlier and better self as his
"little brother" whom he loved and longed for
and sought persistently, but who dropped farther and farther behind at times, until, in moments of darkness, he sometimes feared that he
might lose him forever—Crittenden had clung
to the phrase, and he had let his fancy lead him
to regard this boy as his early and better self—
better far than he had ever been—his little
brother, in a double sense, who drew from him,
besides the love of brother for brother and
father for son, a tenderness that was almost
maternal.

The pike-gate slammed now and the swift
rush of wheels over the bluegrass turf followed;
the barn-gate cracked sharply on the night air
and Crittenden heard him singing, in the boyish,
untrained tenor that is so common in the South,
one of the old-fashioned love-songs that are still
sung with perfect sincerity and without shame
by his people:

"You'll never find another love like mine,
"You'll never find a heart that's half so true."

And then the voice was muffled suddenly. A
little while later he entered the yard-gate and
stopped in the moonlight and, from his window,

Crittenden looked down and watched him. The boy was going through the manual of arms with his buggy-whip, at the command of an imaginary officer, whom, erect and martial, he was apparently looking straight in the eye. Plainly he was a private now. Suddenly he sprang forward and saluted; he was volunteering for some dangerous duty; and then he walked on toward the house. Again he stopped. Apparently he had been promoted now for gallant conduct, for he waved his whip and called out with low, sharp sternness;

"Steady, now! Ready; fire!" And then swinging his hat over his head:

"Double-quick—charge!" After the charge, he sat down for a moment on the stiles, looking up at the moon, and then came on toward the house, singing again:

"You'll never find a man in all this world
Who'll love you half so well as I love you."

And inside, the mother, too, was listening; and she heard the elder brother call the boy into his room and the door close, and she as well knew the theme of their talk as though she could hear all they said. Her sons—even the elder one—did not realize what war was; the boy looked upon it as a frolic. That was the way her two brothers had regarded the old war.

They went with the South, of course, as did her father and her sweetheart. And her sweetheart was the only one who came back, and him she married the third month after the surrender, when he was so sick and wounded that he could hardly stand. Now she must give up all that was left for the North, that had taken nearly all she had.

Was it all to come again—the same long days of sorrow, loneliness, the anxious waiting, waiting, waiting to hear that this one was dead, and that this one was wounded or sick to death— would either come back unharmed? She knew now what her own mother must have suffered, and what it must have cost her to tell her sons what she had told hers that night. Ah, God, was it all to come again?

V

SOME days later a bugle blast started Crittenden from a soldier's cot, when the flaps of
his tent were yellow with the rising sun. Peep-
ing between them, he saw that only one tent was
open. Rivers, as acting-quartermaster, had
been up long ago and gone. That blast was
meant for the private at the foot of the hill,
and Crittenden went back to his cot and
slept on.

The day before he had swept out of the hills
again—out through a blossoming storm of dog-
wood—but this time southward bound. Inci-
dentally, he would see unveiled these statues
that Kentucky was going to dedicate to her
Federal and Confederate dead. He would find
his father's old comrade—little Jerry Carter—
and secure a commission, if possible. Meanwhile, he would drill with Rivers's regiment, as
a soldier of the line.

At sunset he swept into the glory of a Southern
spring and the hallowed haze of an old battle-
field where certain gallant Americans once
fought certain other gallant Americans fiercely

forward and back over some six thousand acres of creek-bottom and wooded hills, and where Uncle Sam was pitching tents for his war-children—children, too—some of them—of those old enemies, but ready to fight together now, and as near shoulder to shoulder as the modern line of battle will allow.

Rivers, bronzed, quick-tempered, and of superb physique, met him at the station.

"You'll come right out to camp with me."

The town was thronged. There were gray slouched hats everywhere with little brass crosses pinned to them—tiny rifles, sabres, cannon—crosses that were not symbols of religion, unless this was a time when the Master's coming meant the sword. Under them were soldiers with big pistols and belts of big, gleaming cartridges—soldiers, white and black, everywhere—swaggering, ogling, and loud of voice, but all good-natured, orderly.

Inside the hotel the lobby was full of officers in uniform, scanning the yellow bulletin-boards, writing letters, chatting in groups; gray veterans of horse, foot, and artillery; company officers in from Western service—quiet young men with bronzed faces and keen eyes, like Rivers's—renewing old friendships and swapping experiences on the plains; subalterns down to the last graduating class from West Point with slim waists, fresh faces, and nothing to swap yet but memories of the old school on the Hudson. In there he saw Grafton again and Lieutenant Sharpe, of the Tenth Colored Cavalry, whom he had seen in the Bluegrass, and Rivers introduced him. He was surprised that Rivers, though a Southerner, had so little feeling on the question of negro soldiers; that many officers in the negro regiments were Southern; that Southerners were preferred because they understood the black man, and, for that reason, could better handle him. Sharpe presented both to his father, Colonel Sharpe, of the infantry, who was taking credit to himself, that, for the first time in his life, he allowed his band to play "Dixie" in camp after the Southerners in Congress had risen up and voted millions for the national defence. Colonel Sharpe spoke with some bitterness and Crittenden wondered. He never dreamed that there was any bitterness on the other side—why? How could a victor feel bitterness for a fallen foe? It was the one word he heard or was to hear about the old war from Federal or ex-Confederate. Indeed, he mistook a short, stout, careless appointee, Major Billings, with his negro servant, his Southern mustache and goatee and his pompous ways, for a genuine Southerner, and the Major, though from Vermont, seemed pleased.

43

But it was to the soldier outside that Crittenden's heart had been drawn, for it was his first stirring sight of the regular of his own land, and the soldier in him answered at once with a thrill. Waiting for Rivers, he stood in the door of the hotel, watching the strong men pass, and by and by he saw three coming down the street, arm in arm. On the edge of the light, the middle one, a low, thick-set, black-browed fellow, pushed his comrades away, fell drunkenly, and slipped loosely to the street, while the two stood above him in disgust. One of them was a mere boy and the other was a giant, with a lean face, so like Lincoln's that Crittenden started when the boy called impatiently:

"Pick him up, Abe."

The tall soldier stooped, and with one hand lifted the drunken man as lightly as though he had been a sack of wool, and the two caught him under the arms again. As they came on, both suddenly let go; the middle one straightened sharply, and all three saluted. Crittenden heard Rivers's voice at his ear:

"Report for this, Reynolds."

And the drunken soldier turned and rather sullenly saluted again.

"You'll come right out to camp with me," repeated Rivers.

And now out at the camp, next morning, a

dozen trumpets were ringing out an emphatic
complaint into Crittenden's sleeping ears:

> "I can't git 'em up,
>   I can't git 'em up,
>   I can't git 'em up in the mornin',
>   I can't git 'em up,
>   I can't git 'em up,
>   I can't git 'em up at all.
> The corporal's worse than the sergeant,
> The sergeant's worse than the lieutenant,
> And the captain is worst of all."

This is as high up, apparently, as the private
dares to go, unless he considers the somnolent
iniquity of the Colonel quite beyond the range
of the bugle. But the pathetic appeal was too
much for Crittenden, and he got up, stepping
into a fragrant foot-bath of cold dew and out to
a dapple gray wash-basin that sat on three
wooden stakes just outside. Sousing his head,
he sniffed in the chill air and, looking below
him, took in, with pure mathematical delight,
the working unit of the army as it came to life.
The very camp was the symbol of order and
system: a low hill, rising from a tiny stream
below him in a series of natural terraces to the
fringe of low pines behind him, and on these
terraces officers and men sitting, according to
rank; the white tepees of the privates and their
tethered horses—camped in column of troops—

stretching up the hill toward him; on the first
terrace above and flanking the columns, the
old-fashioned army tents of company officer and
subaltern and the guidons in line—each captain
with his lieutenants at the head of each company
street; behind them and on the next terrace, the
majors three—each facing the centre of his
squadron.   And highest on top of the hill, and
facing the centre of the regiment, the slate-
coloured tent of the Colonel, commanding every
foot of the camp.

"Yes," said a voice behind him, "and you'll
find it just that way throughout the army."

Crittenden turned in surprise, and the ubiqui-
tous Grafton went on as though the little trick
of thought-reading were too unimportant for
notice.

"Let's go down and take a look at things.
This is my last day," Grafton went on, "and
I'm out early.   I go to Tampa to-morrow."

All the day before, as he travelled, Crittenden
had seen the station thronged with eager country-
men—that must have been the way it was in
the old war, he thought—and swarmed the
thicker the farther he went south.   And now, as
the two started down the hill, he could see in the
dusty road that ran through the old battle-field
Southern interest and sympathy taking visible
shape.   For a hundred miles around, the human

swarm had risen from the earth and was moving toward him on wagon, bicycle, horseback, foot; in omnibus, carriage, cart; in barges on wheels, with projecting additions, and other land-craft beyond classification or description. And the people—the American Southerners; rich whites, whites well-to-do, poor white trash; good country folks, valley farmers; mountaineers —darkies, and the motley feminine horde that the soldier draws the world over—all moving along the road as far as he could see, and interspersed here and there in the long, low cloud of dust with a clanking troop of horse or a red rumbling battery—all coming to see the soldiers —the soldiers!

And the darkies! How they flocked and stared at their soldier-brethren with pathetic worship, dumb admiration, and, here and there, with a look of contemptuous resentment that was most curious. And how those dusky sons of Mars were drinking deep into their broad nostrils the incense wafted to them from hedge and highway.

For a moment Grafton stopped still, looking. "Great!"

Below the Majors' terrace stood an old sergeant, with a gray mustache and a kind, blue eye. Each horse had his nose in a mouth-bag and was contentedly munching corn, while a trooper affectionately curried him from tip of ear to tip of tail.

"Horse ever first and man ever afterward is the trooper's law," said Grafton.

"I suppose you've got the best colonel in the army," he added to the soldier and with a wink at Crittenden.

"Yes, sir," said the guileless old Sergeant, quickly, and with perfect seriousness. "We have, sir, and I'm not sayin' a wor-rd against the rest, sir."

The Sergeant's voice was as kind as his face, and Grafton soon learned that he was called "the Governor" throughout the regiment—that he was a Kentuckian and a sharp-shooter. He had seen twenty-seven years of service, and his ambition had been to become a sergeant of ord-nance. He passed his examination finally, but he was then a little too old. That almost broke the Sergeant's heart, but the hope of a fight, now, was fast healing it.

"I'm from Kentucky, too," said Crittenden. The old soldier turned quickly.

"I knew you were, sir."

This was too much for Grafton. "Now-how-on-earth—" and then he checked himself —it was not his business.

"You're a Crittenden."

"That's right," laughed the Kentuckian.

The Sergeant turned. A soldier came up and asked some trifling question, with a searching look, Grafton observed, at Crittenden. Everyone looked at that man twice, thought Grafton, and he looked again himself. It was his manner, his bearing, the way his head was set on his shoulders, the plastic force of his striking face. But Crittenden saw only that the Sergeant answered the soldier as though he were talking to a superior. He had been watching the men closely—they might be his comrades some day—and, already, had noticed, with increasing surprise, the character of the men whom he saw as common soldiers—young, quiet, and above the average countryman in address and intelligence—and this man's face surprised him still more, as did his bearing. His face was dark, his eye was dark and penetrating and passionate; his mouth was reckless and weak, his build was graceful, and his voice was low and even—the voice of a gentleman; he was the refined type of the Western gentleman-desperado, as Crittenden had imagined it from fiction and hearsay. As the soldier turned away, the old Sergeant saved him the question he was about to ask.

"He used to be an officer."

"Who—how's that?" asked Grafton, scenting "a story."

The old Sergeant checked himself at once, and added cautiously:

"He was a lieutenant in this regiment and he resigned. He just got back to-day, and he has enlisted as a private rather than risk not getting to Cuba at all. But, of course, he'll get his commission back again." The Sergeant's manner fooled neither Grafton nor Crittenden; both respected the old Sergeant's unwillingness to gossip about a man who had been his superior, and Grafton asked no more questions.

There was no idleness in that camp. Each man was busy within and without the conical-walled tents in which the troopers lie like the spokes of a wheel, with heads out like a covey of partridges. Before one tent sat the tall soldier—Abe—and the boy, his comrade, whom Crittenden had seen the night before.

"Where's Reynolds?" asked Crittenden, smiling.

"Guard-house," said the Sergeant, shaking his head.

Not a scrap of waste matter was to be seen anywhere—not a piece of paper—not the faintest odour was perceptible; the camp was as clean as a Dutch kitchen.

"And this is a camp of cavalry, mind you," said Grafton. "Ten minutes after they have broken camp, you won't be able to tell that there has been a man or horse on the ground, except for the fact that it will be packed down hard in places. And I bet you that in a month they won't have three men in the hospital." The old Sergeant nearly blushed with pleasure.

"An' I've got the best captain, too, sir," he said, as they turned away, and Grafton laughed.

"That's the way you'll find it all through the army. Each colonel and each captain is always the best to the soldier, and, by the way," he went on, "do you happen to know about this little United States regular army?"

"Not much."

"I thought so. Germany knows a good deal —England, France, Prussia, Russia—everybody knows but the American and the Spaniard. Just look at these men. They're young, strong, intelligent—bully, good Americans. It's an army of picked men—picked for heart, body, and brain. Almost each man is an athlete. It is the finest body of men on God Almighty's earth to-day, and everybody on earth but the American and the Spaniard knows it. And how this nation has treated them. Think of that miserable Congress—" Grafton waved his hands in impotent rage and ceased—Rivers was calling them from the top of the hill.

So all morning Crittenden watched the regimental unit at work. He took a sabre lesson

51

from the old Sergeant. He visited camps of infantry and artillery and, late that afternoon, he sat on a little wooded hill, where stood four draped, ghost-like statues—watching these units paint pictures on a bigger canvas below him, of the army at work as a whole.

Every green interspace below was thickly dotted with tents and rising spirals of faint smoke; every little plain was filled with soldiers, at drill. Behind him wheeled cannon and caisson and men and horses, splashed with prophetic drops of red, wheeling at a gallop, halting, unlimbering, loading, and firing imaginary shells at imaginary Spaniards—limbering and off with a flash of metal, wheel-spoke and crimson trappings at a gallop again; in the plain below were regiments of infantry, deploying in skirmish-line, advancing by rushes; beyond them sharp-shooters were at target practice, and little bands of recruits and awkward squads were everywhere. In front, rose cloud after cloud of dust, and, under them, surged cloud after cloud of troopers at mounted drill, all making ready for the soldier's work—to kill with mercy and die without complaint. What a picture—what a picture! And what a rich earnest of the sleeping might of the nation behind it all. Just under him was going an "escort of the standard," which he could plainly see. Across the long drill-ground the regiment—it was Rivers's regiment—stood, a solid mass of silent, living statues, and it was a brave sight that came now—that flash of sabres along the long length of the drill-field, like one leaping horizontal flame. It was a regimental acknowledgment of the honour of presentation to the standard, and Crittenden raised his hat gravely in recognition of the same honour, little dreaming that he was soon to follow that standard up a certain Cuban hill.

What a picture!

There the nation was concentrating its power. Behind him that nation was patching up its one great quarrel, and now a gray phantom stalked out of the past to the music of drum and fife, and Crittenden turned sharply to see a little body of men, in queer uniforms, marching through a camp of regulars toward him. They were old boys, and they went rather slowly, but they stepped jauntily and, in their natty old-fashioned caps and old gray jackets pointed into a V-shape behind, they looked jaunty in spite of their years. Not a soldier but paused to look at these men in gray, who marched thus proudly through such a stronghold of blue, and were not ashamed. Not a man joked or laughed or smiled, for all knew that they were old Confederates in butter-nut, and once fighting-men indeed. All knew that these men had fought battles that made scouts and Indian skirmishes and city riots and, perhaps, any battles in store for them with Spain but play by contrast for the tin soldier, upon whom the regular smiles with such mild contempt; that this thin column had seen twice the full muster of the seven thousand strong encamped there melt away upon that very battlefield in a single day. And so the little remnant of gray marched through an atmosphere of profound respect, and on through a mist of memories to the rocky little point where the Federal Virginian Thomas—"The Rock of Chickamauga"—stood against seventeen fierce assaults of hill-swarming demons in butter-nut, whose desperate valour has hardly a parallel on earth, unless it then and there found its counterpart in the desperate courage of the brothers in name and race whose lives they sought that day. They were bound to a patriotic love-feast with their old enemies in blue—these men in gray— to hold it on the hill around the four bronze statues that Crittenden's State was putting up to her sons who fought on one or the other side on that one battle-field, and Crittenden felt a clutch at his heart and his eyes filled when the tattered old flag of the stars and bars trembled toward him. Under its folds rode the spirit of gallant fraternity—a little, old man with a grizzled beard and with stars on his shoulders, his hands folded on the pommel of his saddle, his eyes lifted dreamily upward—they called him the "bee-hunter," from that habit of his in the old war—his father's old comrade, little Jerry Carter. That was the man Crittenden had come South to see. Behind came a carriage, in which sat a woman in widow's weeds and a tall girl in gray. He did not need to look again to see that it was Judith, and, motionless, he stood where he was throughout the ceremony, until he saw the girl lift her hand and the veil fall away from the bronze symbols of the soldier that was in her fathers and in his—stood resolutely still until the gray figure disappeared and the veterans, blue and gray intermingled, marched away. The little General was the last to leave, and he rode slowly, as if overcome with memories. Crittenden took off his hat and, while he hesitated, hardly knowing whether to make himself known or not, the little man caught sight of him and stopped short.

"Why—why, bless my soul, aren't you Tom Crittenden's son?"

"Yes, sir," said Crittenden.

"I knew it. Bless me, I was thinking of him just that moment—naturally enough—and you startled me. I thought it was Tom himself." He grasped the Kentuckian's hand warmly.

"Yes," he said, studying his face. "You look

just as he did when we courted and camped and fought together." The tone of his voice moved Crittenden deeply. "And you are going to the war—good—good! Your father would be with me right now if he were alive. Come to see me right away. I may go to Tampa any day." And, as he rode away, he stopped again.

"Of course you have a commission in the Legion."

"No, sir. I didn't ask for one. I was afraid the Legion might not get to Cuba." The General smiled.

"Well, come to see me"—he smiled again— "we'll see—we'll see!" and he rode on with his hands still folded on the pommel of his saddle and his eyes still lifted, dreamily, upward.

It was guard-mount and sunset when Crittenden, with a leaping heart, reached Rivers's camp. The band was just marching out with a corps of trumpeters, when a crash of martial music came across the hollow from the camp on the next low hill, followed by cheers, which ran along the road and were swollen into a mighty shouting when taken up by the camp at the foot of the hill. Through the smoke and faint haze of the early evening, moved a column of infantry into sight, headed by a band.

> "Tramp, tramp, tramp,
> The boys are marching!"

56

Along the brow of the hill, and but faintly seen through the smoky haze, came the pendulum-like swing of rank after rank of sturdy legs, with guidons fluttering along the columns and big, ghostly army wagons rumbling behind. Up started the band at the foot of the hill with a rousing march, and up started every band along the line, and through madly cheering soldiers swung the regiment on its way to Tampa —magic word, hope of every chafing soldier left behind—Tampa, the point of embarkation for the little island where waited death or glory.

Rivers was deeply dejected.

"Don't you join any regiment yet," he said to Crittenden; "you may get hung up here all summer till the war is over. If you want to get into the fun for sure—wait. Go to Tampa and wait. You might come here, or go there, and drill and watch for your chance." Which was the conclusion Crittenden had already reached for himself.

The sun sank rapidly now. Dusk fell swiftly, and the pines began their nightly dirge for the many dead who died under them five and thirty years ago. They had a new and ominous chant now to Crittenden—a chant of premonition for the strong men about him who were soon to follow them. Camp-fires began to glow out of

57

the darkness far and near over the old battle-field.

Around a little fire on top of the hill, and in front of the Colonel's tent, sat the Colonel, with kind Irish face, Irish eye, and Irish wit of tongue. Near him the old Indian-fighter, Chaffee, with strong brow, deep eyes, long jaw, firm mouth, strong chin—the long, lean face of a thirteenth century monk who was quick to doff cowl for helmet. While they told war-stories, Crittenden sat in silence with the majors three, and Willings, the surgeon (whom he was to know better in Cuba), and listened. Every now and then a horse would loom from the darkness, and a visiting officer would swing into the light, and everybody would say:

"How!"

There is no humour in that monosyllable of good cheer throughout the United States Army, and with Indian-like solemnity they said it, tin cup in hand,

"How!"

Once it was Lawton, tall, bronzed, commanding, taciturn—but fluent when he did speak—or Kent, or Sumner, or little Jerry Carter himself. And once, a soldier stepped into the circle of firelight, his heels clicking sharply together; and Crittenden thought an uneasy movement ran around the group, and that the younger men

looked furtively up as though to take their cue
from the Colonel. It was the soldier who had
been an officer once. The Colonel showed not
a hint of consciousness, nor did the impassive
soldier to anybody but Crittenden, and with him
it may have been imagination that made him
think that once, when the soldier let his eye
flash quite around the group, he flushed slightly
when he met Crittenden's gaze. Rivers shrugged
his shoulders when Crittenden asked about him
later.

"Black sheep . . . well-educated, brave,
well-born most likely, came up from the ranks,
. . . won a commission as sergeant fighting
Indians, but always in trouble—gambling, fighting, and so forth. Somebody in Washington
got him a lieutenancy, and while the commission
was on its way to him out West he got into a
bar-room brawl. He resigned then, and left
the army. He was gentleman enough to do
that. Now he's back. The type is common in
the army, and they often come back. I expect
he has decency enough to want to get killed.
If he has, maybe he'll come out a captain
yet."

By and by came "tattoo," and finally far
away a trumpet sounded "taps"; then another
and another and another still. At last, when
all were through, "taps" rose once more out of

the darkness to the left. This last trumpeter had waited—he knew his theme and knew his power. The rest had simply given the command:

"Lights out!"

Lights out of the soldier's camp, they said. Lights out of the soldier's life, said this one, sadly; and out of Crittenden's life just now something that once was dearer than life itself.

"Love, good-night."

Such the trumpet meant to one poet, and such it meant to many another than Crittenden, doubtless, when he stretched himself on his cot —thinking of Judith there that afternoon, and seeing her hand lift to pull away the veil from the statues again. So it had always been with him. One touch of her hand and the veil that hid his better self parted, and that self stepped forth victorious. It had been thickening, fold on fold, a long while now; and now, he thought sternly, the rending must be done, and should be done with his own hands. And then he would go back to thinking of her as he saw her last in the Bluegrass. And he wondered what that last look and smile of hers could mean. Later, he moved in his sleep—dreaming of that brave column marching for Tampa—with his mind's eye on the flag at the head of the regiment, and a thrill about his heart that waked him. And he remembered that it was the first time he had ever had any sensation about the flag of his own land. But it had come to him—awake and asleep—and it was genuine.

VI

IT was mid-May now, and the leaves were full and their points were drooping toward the earth. The woods were musical with the cries of blackbirds as Crittenden drove toward the pike-gate, and the meadow was sweet with the love-calls of larks. The sun was fast nearing the zenith, and air and earth were lusty with life. Already the lane, lined with locust-trees, brambles, wild rose-bushes, and young elders, was fragrant with the promise of unborn flowers, and the turnpike, when he neared town, was soft with the dust of many a hoof and wheel that had passed over it toward the haze of smoke which rose over the first recruiting camp in the State for the Spanish war. There was a big crowd in the lovely woodland over which hung the haze, and the music of horn and drum came forth to Crittenden's ears even that far away, and Raincrow raised head and tail and quickened his pace proudly.

For a week he had drilled at Chickamauga. He had done the work of a plain soldier, and he liked it—liked his temporary comrades, who were frankly men to men with him, in spite of his friendship with their superiors on top of the hill. To the big soldier, Abe Long, the wag of the regiment, he had been drawn with genuine affection. He liked Abe's bunkie, the boy Sanders, who was from Maine, while Abe was a Westerner—the lineal descendant in frame, cast of mind, and character of the border backwoodsman of the Revolution. Reynolds was a bully, and Crittenden all but had trouble with him; for he bullied the boy Sanders when Abe was not around, and bullied the "rookies." Abe seemed to have little use for him, but as he had saved the big soldier's life once in an Indian fight, Abe stuck to him, in consequence, loyally. But Blackford, the man who had been an officer once, had interested him most; perhaps, because Blackford showed peculiar friendliness for him at once. From Washington, Crittenden had heard not a word; nor from General Carter, who had left Chickamauga before he could see him again. If, within two days more, no word came, Crittenden had made up his mind to go to Tampa, where the little General was, and where Rivers's regiment had been ordered, and drill again and, as Rivers advised, await his chance.

The camp was like some great picnic or political barbecue, with the smoking trenches, the burgoo, and the central feast of beef and mutton left out. Everywhere country folks were gath-

ering up fragments of lunch on the thick grass,
or strolling past the tents of the soldiers, or stopping before the Colonel's pavilion to look upon
the martial young gentlemen who composed his
staff, their beautiful horses, and the Colonel's
beautiful guests from the river city—the big
town of the State. Everywhere were young
soldiers in twos and threes keeping step, to be
sure, but with eyes anywhere but to the front;
groups lying on the ground, chewing blades of
bluegrass, watching gretty girls pass, and
lounging lazily; groups to one side, but by no
means out of sight, throwing dice or playing
"craps"—the game dear to the darkey's heart.
On the outskirts were guards to gently challenge
the visitor, but not very stern sentinels were
they. As Crittenden drove in, he saw one pacing
ing a shady beat with a girl on his arm. And
later, as he stood by his buggy, looking around
with an amused sense of the playful contrast it all
was to what he had seen at Chickamauga, he
saw another sentinel brought to a sudden halt
by a surprised exclamation from a girl, who was
being shown through the camp by a strutting
lieutenant. The sentinel was Basil and Phyllis
was the girl.

"Why, isn't that Basil?" she asked in an
amazed tone—amazed because Basil did not
speak to her, but grinned silently.

"Why, it is Basil; why—why," and she turned helplessly from private to officer and back again. "Can't you speak to me, Basil?"

Basil grinned again sheepishly.

"Yes," he said, answering her, but looking straight at his superior, "I can if the Lieutenant there will let me." Phyllis was indignant.

"Let you!" she said, witheringly; and she turned on the hapless tyrant at her side.

"Now, don't you go putting on airs, just because you happen to have been in the Legion a little longer than *some* people. Of course, I'm going to speak to my friends. I don't care where they are or what they happen to be at the time, or who happens to think himself over them."

And she walked up to the helpless sentinel with her hand outstretched, while the equally helpless Lieutenant got very red indeed, and Basil shifted his gun to a very unmilitary position and held out his hand.

"Let me see your gun, Basil," she added, and the boy obediently handed it over to her, while the little Lieutenant turned redder still.

"You go to the guard-house for that, Crittenden," he said, quietly. "Don't you know you oughtn't to give up your gun to anybody except your commanding officer?"

"Does he, indeed?" said the girl, just as

quietly. "Well, I'll see the Colonel." And Basil saluted soberly, knowing there was no guard-house for him that night.

"Anyhow," she added, "I'm the commanding officer here." And then the gallant lieutenant saluted too.

"You are, indeed," he said; and Phyllis turned to give Basil a parting smile.

Crittenden followed them to the Colonel's tent, which had a raised floor and the good cheer of cigar-boxes, and of something under his cot that looked like a champagne-basket; and he smiled to think of Chaffee's Spartan-like outfit at Chickamauga. Every now and then a soldier would come up with a complaint, and the Colonel would attend to him personally.

It was plain that the old ex-Confederate was the father of the regiment, and was beloved as such; and Crittenden was again struck with the contrast it all was to what he had just seen, knowing well, however, that the chief difference was in the spirit in which regular and volunteer approached the matter in hand. With one, it was a business pure and simple, to which he was trained. With the other, it was a lark at first, but business it soon would be, and a dashing business at that. There was the same crowd before the tent—Judith, who greeted him with gracious frankness, but with a humorous

light in her eye that set him again to wondering;
and Phyllis and Phyllis's mother, Mrs. Stanton,
who no sooner saw Crittenden than she furtively
looked at Judith with a solicitude that was maternal and significant.

There can be no better hot-bed of sentiment
than the mood of man and woman when the
man is going to war; and if Mrs. Stanton had not
shaken that nugget of wisdom from her memories of the old war, she would have known it
anyhow, for she was blessed with a perennial
sympathy for the heart-troubles of the young,
and she was as quick to apply a remedy to the
children of other people as she was to her own,
whom, by the way, she cured, one by one, as
they grew old enough to love and suffer, and
learn through suffering what it was to be happy.
And how other mothers wondered how it was
all done! In truth, her method—if she had a
conscious method—was as mysterious and as
sure as is the way of nature; and one could no
more catch her nursing a budding passion here
and there than one could catch nature making
the bluegrass grow. Everybody saw the result;
nobody saw just how it was done. That afternoon an instance was at hand. Judith wanted
to go home, and Mrs. Stanton, who had brought
her to camp, wanted to go to town. Phyllis,
too, wanted to go home, and her wicked little

brother, Walter, who had brought her, climbed into Basil's brake before her eyes, and, making a face at her, disappeared in a cloud of dust. Of course, neither of the brothers nor the two girls knew what was going on, but, a few minutes later, there was Basil pleading with Mrs. Stanton to let him take Phyllis home, and there was Crittenden politely asking the privilege of taking Judith into his buggy. The girl looked embarrassed, but when Mrs. Stanton made a gracious feint of giving up her trip to town, Judith even more graciously declined to allow her, and, with a smile to Crittenden, as though he were a conscious partner in her effort to save Mrs. Stanton trouble, gave him her hand and was helped into the smart trap, with its top pressed flat, its narrow seat and a high-headed, high-reined, half-thoroughbred restive between the slender shafts; and a moment later, smiled a good-by to the placid lady, who, with a sigh that was half an envious memory, half the throb of a big, kind heart, turned to her own carriage, assuring herself that it really was imperative for her to drive to town, if for no other reason than to see that her mischievous boy got out of town with the younger Crittenden's brake.

Judith and Crittenden were out of the push of cart, carriage, wagon, and street-car now, and out of the smoke and dust of the town, and

Crittenden pulled his horse down to a slow trot. The air was clear and fragrant and restful. So far, the two had spoken scarcely a dozen words. Crittenden was embarrassed—he hardly knew why—and Judith saw it, and there was a suppressed smile at the corners of her mouth which Crittenden did not see.

"It's too bad."

Crittenden turned suddenly.

"It's a great pleasure."

"For which you have Mrs. Stanton to thank. You would have got it for yourself five—dear me; is it possible ?—five years ago."

"Seven years ago," corrected Crittenden, grimly. "I was more self-indulgent seven years ago than I am now."

"And the temptation was greater then."

The smile at her mouth twitched her lips faintly, and still Crittenden did not see; he was too serious, and he kept silent.

The clock-like stroke of the horse's high-lifted feet came sharply out on the hard road. The cushioned springs under them creaked softly now and then, and the hum of the slender, glittering spokes was noiseless and drowsy.

"You haven't changed much," said Judith, "except for the better."

"You haven't changed at all. You couldn't —for better or worse."

Judith smiled dreamily and her eyes were looking backward—very far backward. Suddenly they were shot with mischief.

"Why, you really don't seem to—" she hesitated—"to like me any more."

"I really don't—" Crittenden, too, hesitated —"don't like you any more—not as I did."

"You wrote me that."

"Yes."

The girl gave a low laugh. How often he had played this harmless little part. But there was a cool self-possession about him that she had never seen before. She had come home, prepared to be very nice to him, and she was finding it easy.

"And you never answered," said Crittenden.

"No; and I don't know why."

The birds were coming from shade and picket —for midday had been warm—into the fields and along the hedges, and were fluttering from one fence-rail to another ahead of them and piping from the bushes by the wayside and the top of young weeds.

"You wrote that you were—'getting over it.' In the usual way?"

Crittenden glanced covertly at Judith's face. A mood in her like this always made him uneasy.

"Not in the usual way; I don't think it's usual. I hope not."

70

"How, then?"

"Oh, pride, absence—deterioration and other things."

"Why, then?"

Judith's head was leaning backward, her eyes were closed, but her face seemed perfectly serious.

"You told me to get over it."

"Did I?"

Crittenden did not deign to answer this, and Judith was silent a long while. Then her eyes opened; but they were looking backward again, and she might have been talking to herself.

"I'm wondering," she said, "whether any woman ever really meant that when she said it to a man whom she—" Crittenden turned quickly—"whom she liked," added Judith as though she had not seen his movement. "She may think it her duty to say it; she may say it because it is her duty; but in her heart, I suppose, she wants him to keep on loving her just the same—if she likes him—" Judith paused— "even more than a very little. That's very selfish, but I'm afraid it's true."

And Judith sighed helplessly.

"I think you made it little enough that time," laughed Crittenden. "Are you still afraid of giving me too much hope?"

"I am afraid of nothing—now."

"Thank you You were ever too much concerned about me."

"I was. Other men may have found the fires of my conscience smouldering sometimes, but they were always ablaze whenever you came near. I liked you better than the rest—better than all——"

Crittenden's heart gave a faint throb and he finished the sentence for her.

"But one."

"But one."

And that one had been unworthy, and Judith had sent him adrift. She had always been frank with Crittenden. That much he knew and no more—not even the man's name; but how he had wondered who and where and what manner of man he was! And how he had longed to see him!

They were passing over a little bridge in a hollow where a cool current of air struck them and the freshened odour of moistening green things in the creek-bed—the first breath of the night that was still below the cloudy horizon.

"Deterioration," said Judith, almost sharply. "What did you mean by that?"

Crittenden hesitated, and she added:

"Go on; we are no longer children."

"Oh, it was nothing, or everything, just as

you look at it. I made a discovery soon after you went away. I found that when I fell short of the standard you"—Crittenden spoke slowly —"had set for me, I got at least mental relief. I *couldn't* think of you until—until I had recovered myself again."

"So you——"

"I used the discovery."

"That was weak."

"It was deliberate."

"Then it was criminal."

"Both, if you wish; but credit me with at least the strength to confess and the grace to be ashamed. But I'm beginning all over again now—by myself."

He was flipping at one shaft with the cracker of his whip and not looking at her, and Judith kept silent; but she was watching his face.

"It's time," he went on, with slow humour. "So far, I've just missed being what I should have been; doing what I should have done—by a hair's breadth. I did pretty well in college, but thereafter, when things begin to count! Law? I never got over the humiliation of my first ridiculous failure. Business? I made a fortune in six weeks, lost it in a month, and was lucky to get out without having to mortgage a farm. Politics? Wharton won by a dozen votes. I just missed being what my brother is

73

now—I missed winning you—everything! Think of it! I am five feet eleven and three-quarters, when I should have been full six feet. I am the first Crittenden to fall under the line in a century. I have been told"—he smiled—"that I have missed being handsome. There again I believe I overthrow family tradition. My youth is going—to no purpose, so far—and it looks as though I were going to miss life hereafter as well as here, since, along with everything else, I have just about missed faith."

He was quite sincere and unsparing, but had Judith been ten years older, she would have laughed outright. As it was, she grew sober and sympathetic and, like a woman, began to wonder, for the millionth time, perhaps, how far she had been to blame.

"The comfort I have is that I have been, and still am, honest with myself. I haven't done what I ought not and then tried to persuade myself that it was right. I always knew it was wrong, and I did it anyhow. And the hope I have is that, like the man in Browning's poem, I believe I always try to get up again, no matter how often I stumble. I sha'n't give up hope until I am willing to lie still. And I guess, after all—" he lifted his head suddenly—"I haven't missed being a man."

"And a gentleman," added Judith gently.

"According to the old standard—no." Crittenden paused.

The sound of buggy wheels and a fast-trotting horse rose behind them. Raincrow lifted his head and quickened his pace, but Crittenden pulled him in as Basil and Phyllis swept by. The two youngsters were in high spirits, and the boy shook his whip back and the girl her handkerchief—both crying something which neither Judith nor Crittenden could understand. Far behind was the sound of another horse's hoofs, and Crittenden, glancing back, saw his political enemy—Wharton—a girl by his side, and coming at full speed. At once he instinctively gave half the road, and Raincrow, knowing what that meant, shot out his feet and Crittenden tightened the reins, not to check, but to steady him. The head of the horse behind he could just see, but he went on talking quietly.

"I love that boy," pointing with his whip ahead. "Do you remember that passage I once read you in Stevenson about his 'little brother'?"

Judith nodded.

The horse behind was creeping up now, and his open nostrils were visible past the light hair blowing about Judith's neck. Crittenden spoke one quiet word to his own horse, and Judith saw the leaders of his wrist begin to stand out as

Raincrow settled into the long reach that had sent his sire a winner under many a string.

"Well, I know what he meant—that boy never will. And that is as a man should be. The hope of the race isn't in this buggy—it has gone on before with Phyllis and Basil."

Once the buggy wheels ran within an inch of a rather steep bank, and straight ahead was a short line of broken limestone so common on bluegrass turnpikes, but Judith had the Southern girl's trust and courage, and seemed to notice the reckless drive as little as did Crittenden, who made the wheels straddle the stones, when the variation of an inch or two would have lamed his horse and overturned them.

"Yes, they are as frank as birds in their love-making, and they will marry with as little question as birds do when they nest. They will have a house full of children—I have heard her mother say that was her ambition and the ambition she had for her children; and they will live a sane, wholesome, useful, happy life."

The buggy behind had made a little spurt, and the horses were almost neck and neck. Wharton looked ugly, and the black-eyed girl with fluffy black hair was looking behind Judith's head at Crittenden and was smiling. Not once had Judith turned her head, even to see who they were. Crittenden hardly knew

" Go on ! " said Judith.

whether she was conscious of the race, but they were approaching her gate now and he found out.

"Shall I turn in?" he asked.

"Go on," said Judith.

There was a long, low hill before them, and up that Crittenden let Raincrow have his full speed for the first time. The panting nostrils of the other horse fell behind—out of sight—out of hearing.

"And if he doesn't get back from the war, she will mourn for him sincerely for a year or two and then——"

"Marry someone else."

"Why not?"

That was what she had so often told him to do, and now he spoke as though it were quite possible—even for him; and she was both glad and a little resentful.

At the top of the hill they turned. The enemy was trotting leisurely up the slope, having given up the race earlier than they knew. Judith's face was flushed.

"I don't think you are so very old," she said.

Crittenden laughed, and took off his hat very politely when they met the buggy, but Wharton looked surly. The girl with the black hair looked sharply at Judith, and then again at Crittenden, and smiled. She must have cared little for her companion, Judith thought, or something for Crittenden, and yet she knew that most women smiled at Crittenden, even when they did not know him very well. Still she asked: "And the other things—you meant other women?"

"Yes, and no."

"Why no?"

"Because I have deceived nobody—not even myself—and Heaven knows I tried that hard enough."

"That was one?" she added, smiling.

"I thought you knew me better than to ask such a question."

Again Judith smiled—scanning him closely.

"No, you aren't so very old—nor world-weary, after all."

"No?"

"No. And you have strong hands—and wrists. And your eyes are—" she seemed almost embarrassed—"are the eyes of a good man, in spite of what you say about yourself; and I would trust them. And it was very fine in you to talk as you did when we were tearing up that hill a moment ago."

Crittenden turned with a start of surprise.

"Oh," he said, with unaffected carelessness. "You didn't seem to be very nervous."

"I trusted you."

78

Crittenden had stopped to pull the self-opening gate, and he drove almost at a slow walk through the pasture toward Judith's home. The sun was reddening through the trees now. The whole earth was moist and fragrant, and the larks were singing their last songs for that happy day.   Judith was quite serious now.

"Do you know, I was glad to hear you say that you had got over your old feeling for me. I feel so relieved.   I have always felt so responsible for your happiness, but I don't now, and it is *such* a relief.   Now you will go ahead and marry some lovely girl and you will be happy and I shall be happier—seeing it and knowing it."

Crittenden shook his head.

"No," he said, "something seems to have gone out of me, never to come back."

There was nobody in sight to open the yard gate, and Crittenden drove to the stiles, where he helped Judith out and climbed back into his buggy.

Judith turned in surprise.   "Aren't you coming in?"

"I'm afraid I haven't time."

"Oh, yes, you have."

A negro boy was running from the kitchen.

"Hitch Mr. Crittenden's horse," she said, and Crittenden climbed out obediently and followed her to the porch, but she did not sit down outside. She went on into the parlour and threw open the window to let the last sunlight in, and sat by it looking at the west.

For a moment Crittenden watched her. He never realized before how much simple physical beauty she had, nor did he realize the significance of the fact that never until now had he observed it. She had been a spirit before; now she was a woman as well. But he did note that if he could have learned only from Judith, he would never have known that he even had wrists or eyes until that day; and yet he was curiously unstirred by the subtle change in her. He was busied with his own memories.

"And I know it can never come back," he said, and he went on thinking as he looked at her. "I wonder if you can know what it is to have somebody such a part of your life that you never hear a noble strain of music, never read a noble line of poetry, never catch a high mood from nature, nor from your own best thoughts —that you do not imagine her by your side to share your pleasure in it all; that you make no effort to better yourself or help others; that you do nothing of which she could approve, that you are not thinking of her—that really she is not the inspiration of it all. That doesn't come but once. Think of having somebody so linked with your life, with what is highest and best in you, that, when the hour of temptation comes and overcomes, you are not able to think of her through very shame. I wonder if *he* loved you that way. I wonder if you know what such love is."

"It never comes but once," he said, in a low tone, that made Judith turn suddenly. Her eyes looked as if they were not far from tears.

A tiny star showed in the pink glow over the west—

"Starlight, star bright!"

"Think of it. For ten years I never saw the first star without making the same wish for you and me. Why," he went on, and stopped suddenly with a little shame at making the confession even to himself, and at the same time with an impersonal wonder that such a thing could be, "I used to pray for you always—when I said my prayers—actually. And sometimes even now, when I'm pretty hopeless and helpless and moved by some memory, the old prayer comes back unconsciously and I find myself repeating your name."

For the moment he spoke as though not only that old love, but she who had caused it, were dead, and the tone of his voice made her shiver.

And the suffering he used to get—the suffering from trifles—the foolish suffering from silly trifles!

He turned now, for he heard Judith walking toward him. She was looking him straight in the eyes and was smiling strangely.

"I'm going to make you love me as you used to love me."

Her lips were left half parted from the whisper, and he could have stooped and kissed her—something that never in his life had he done—he knew that—but the old reverence came back from the past to forbid him, and he merely looked down into her eyes, flushing a little.

"Yes," she said, gently. "And I think you are just tall enough."

In a flash her mood changed, and she drew his head down until she could just touch his forehead with her lips. It was a sweet bit of motherliness—no more—and Crittenden understood and was grateful.

"Go home now," she said.

VII

AT Tampa—the pomp and circumstance of war.

A gigantic hotel, brilliant with lights, music, flowers, women; halls and corridors filled with bustling officers, uniformed from empty straps to stars; volunteer and regular—easily distinguished by the ease of one and the new and conscious erectness of the other; adjutants, millionaire aids, civilian inspectors; gorgeous attachés —English, German, Swedish, Russian, Prussian, Japanese—each wondrous to the dazzled republican eye; Cubans with cigarettes, Cubans—little and big, warlike, with the tail of the dark eye ever womanward, brave with machétes; on the divans Cuban senoritas—refugees at Tampa— dark-eyed, of course, languid of manner, to be sure, and with the eloquent fan, ever present, omnipotent—shutting and closing, shutting and closing, like the wings of a gigantic butterfly; adventurers, adventuresses; artists, photographers; correspondents by the score—female correspondents; story writers, novelists, real war correspondents, and real draughtsmen—artists, indeed; and a host of lesser men with spurs yet to win—all crowding the hotel day and night, night and day.

And outside, to the sea—camped in fine white sand dust, under thick stars and a hot sun—soldiers, soldiers everywhere, lounging through the streets and the railway stations, overrunning the suburbs; drilling—horseback and on foot—through clouds of sand; drilling at skirmish over burnt sedge-grass and stunted and charred pine woods; riding horses into the sea, and plunging in themselves like truant school-boys. In the bay a fleet of waiting transports, and all over dock, camp, town, and hotel an atmosphere of fierce unrest and of eager longing to fill those wooden hulks, rising and falling with such maddening patience on the tide, and to be away. All the time, meanwhile, soldiers coming in—more and more soldiers—in freight-box, day-coach, and palace-car.

That night, in the hotel, Grafton and Crittenden watched the crowd from a divan of red plush, Grafton chatting incessantly. Around them moved and sat the women of the "House of the Hundred Thousand"—officers' wives and daughters and sisters and sweethearts and army widows—claiming rank and giving it more or less consciously, according to the rank of the man whom they represented. The big man with the monocle and the suit of towering white from foot to crown was the English naval attaché. He stalked through the hotel as though he had the British Empire at his back.

"And he has, too," said Grafton. "You ought to see him go down the steps to the café. The door is too low for him. Other tall people bend forward—he always rears back."

And the picturesque little fellow with the helmet was the English military attaché. Crittenden had seen him at Chickamauga, and Grafton said they would hear of him in Cuba. The Prussian was handsome, and a Count. The big, boyish blond was a Russian, and a Prince, as was the quiet, modest, little Japanese —a mighty warrior in his own country. And the Swede, the polite, the exquisite!

"He wears a mustache guard. I offered him a cigar. He saluted: 'Thank you,' he said. 'Nevare I schmoke.'"

"They are the pets of the expedition," Grafton went on, "they and that war-like group of correspondents over there. They'll go down on the flag-ship, while we nobodies will herd together on one boat. But we'll all be on the same footing when we get there."

Just then a big man, who was sitting on the next divan twisting his mustache and talking chiefly with his hands, rolled up and called Grafton.

"Huh!" he said.

"Huh!" mimicked Grafton.

"You don't know much about the army."

"Six weeks ago I couldn't tell a doughboy officer from a cavalryman by the stripe down his legs."

The big man smiled with infinite pity and tolerance.

"Therefore," said Grafton, "I shall not pass judgment, deliver expert military opinions, and decide how the campaign ought to be conducted —well, maybe for some days yet."

"You've got to. You must have a policy— a Policy. I'll give you one."

And he began—favoring monosyllables, dashes, exclamation points, pauses for pantomime, Indian sign language, and heys, huhs, and humphs that were intended to fill out sentences and round up elaborate argument.

"There is a lot any damn fool can say, of course, hey? But you mustn't say it, huh? Give 'em hell afterward." (Pantomime.) "That's right, ain't it? Understand? Regular army all right." (Sign language.) "These damn fools outside—volunteers, politicians, hey? Had best army in the world at the close of the old war, see? Best equipped, you understand, huh? Con-

gress" (violent Indian sign language) "wanted
to squash it—to squash it—that's right, you
understand, huh? Cut it down—cut it down,
see? Illustrate: Wanted 18,000 mules for this
push, got 2,000, see? Same principle all
through; see? That's right! No good to say
anything now—people think you complain of
the regular army, huh? Mustn't say anything
now—give 'em hell afterward—understand?"
(More sign language.) "Hell afterward. All
right now, got your policy, go ahead."

Grafton nodded basely, and without a smile:
"Thanks, old man—thanks. It's very lucid."

A little later Crittenden saw the stout civilian,
Major Billings, fairly puffing with pride, excitement, and a fine uniform of khaki, whom he
had met at Chickamauga; and Willings, the surgeon; and Chaffee, now a brigadier; and Lawton,
soon to command a division; and, finally, little
Jerry Carter, quiet, unassuming, dreamy, slight,
old, but active, and tough as hickory. The
little general greeted Crittenden like a son.

"I was sorry not to see you again at Chickamauga, but I started here next day. I have
just written you that there was a place on my
staff for you or your brother—or for any son of
your father and my friend. I'll write to Washington for you to-night, and you can report for
duty whenever you please."

The little man made the astounding proposition as calmly as though he were asking the Kentuckian to a lunch of bacon and hardtack, and Crittenden flushed with gratitude and his heart leaped—his going was sure now. Before he could stammer out his thanks, the general was gone. Just then Rivers, who, to his great joy, had got at least that far, sat down by him. He was much depressed. His regiment was going, but two companies would be left behind. His colonel talked about sending him back to Kentucky to bring down some horses, and he was afraid to go.

"To think of being in the army as long as I have been, just for this fight. And to think of being left here in this hell-hole all summer, and missing all the fun in Cuba, not to speak of the glory and the game. We haven't had a war for so long that glory will come easy now, and anybody who does anything will be promoted. But it's missing the fight—the fight—that worries me," and Rivers shook his head from side to side dejectedly. "If my company goes, I'm all right; but if it doesn't, there is no chance for me if I go away. I shall lose my last chance of slipping in somewhere. I swear I'd rather go as a private than not at all."

This idea gave Crittenden a start, and made him on the sudden very thoughtful.

88

"Can you get me in as a private at the last minute?" he asked presently.

"Yes," said Rivers, quickly, "and I'll telegraph you in plenty of time, so that you can get back."

Crittenden smiled, for Rivers's plan was plain, but he was thinking of a plan of his own.

Meanwhile, he drilled as a private each day. He was ignorant of the Krag-Jorgensen, and at Chickamauga he had made such a laughable exhibition of himself that the old Sergeant took him off alone one day, and when they came back the Sergeant was observed to be smiling broadly. At the first target practice thereafter, Crittenden stood among the first men of the company, and the captain took mental note of him as a sharpshooter to be remembered when they got to Cuba. With the drill he had little trouble— being a natural-born horseman—so one day, when a trooper was ill, he was allowed to take the sick soldier's place and drill with the regiment. That day his trouble with Reynolds came. All the soldiers were free and easy of speech and rather reckless with epithets, and, knowing how little was meant, Crittenden merely remonstrated with the bully and smilingly asked him to desist.

"Suppose I don't?"

Crittenden smiled again and answered nothing, and Reynolds mistook his silence for timidity. At right wheel, a little later, Crittenden squeezed the bully's leg, and Reynolds cursed him. He might have passed that with a last warning, but, as they wheeled again, he saw Reynolds kick Sanders so violently that the boy's eyes filled with tears. He went straight for the soldier as soon as the drill was over.

"Put up your guard."

"Aw, go to——"

The word was checked at his lips by Crittenden's fist. In a rage, Reynolds threw his hand behind him, as though he would pull his revolver, but his wrist was caught by sinewy fingers from behind. It was Blackford, smiling into his purple face.

"Hold on!" he said, "save that for a Spaniard."

At once, as a matter of course, the men led the way behind the tents, and made a ring— Blackford, without a word, acting as Crittenden's second. Reynolds was the champion bruiser of the regiment and a boxer of no mean skill, and Blackford looked anxious.

"Worry him, and he'll lose his head. Don't try to do him up too quickly."

Reynolds was coarse, disdainful, and triumphant, but he did not look quite so confident when Crittenden stripped and showed a white body, closely jointed at shoulder and elbow and at

knee and thigh, and closely knit with steel-like
tendons.   The long muscles of his back slipped
like eels under his white skin.   Blackford looked
relieved.

"Do you know the game?"

"A little."

"Worry him and wait till he loses his head—
remember, now."

"All right," said Crittenden, cheerfully, and
turned and faced Reynolds, smiling.

"Gawd," said Abe Long.   "He's one o' the
fellows that laugh when they're fightin'.   They're
worse than the cryin' sort—a sight worse."

The prophecy in the soldier's tone soon came
true.   The smile never left Crittenden's face,
even when it was so bruised up that smiling was
difficult; but the onlookers knew that the spirit
of the smile was still there.   Blackford himself
was smiling now.   Crittenden struck but for one
place at first—Reynolds's nose, which was naturally large and red, because he could reach it
every time he led out.   The nose swelled and
still reddened, and Reynolds's small black eyes
narrowed and flamed with a wicked light.   He
fought with his skill at first, but those maddening taps on his nose made him lose his head
altogether in the sixth round, and he senselessly
rushed at Crittenden with lowered head, like a
sheep.   Crittenden took him sidewise on his

jaw as he came, and stepped aside. Reynolds pitched to the ground heavily, and Crittenden bent over him.

"You let that boy alone," he said, in a low voice, and then aloud and calmly:

"I don't like this, but it's in deference to your customs. I don't call names, and I allow nobody to call me names; and if I have another fight," Reynolds was listening now, "it won't be with my fists."

"Well, Mister Man from Kentucky," said Abe, "I'd a damn sight ruther you'd use a club on me than them fists; but there's others of us who don't call names, and ain't called names; and some of us ain't easy skeered, neither."

"I wasn't threatening," said Crittenden, quickly, "but I have heard a good deal of that sort of thing flying around, and I don't want to get into this sort of a thing again." He looked steadily at the soldier, but the eye of Abraham Long quailed not at all. Instead, a smile broke over his face.

"I got a drink waitin' fer you," he said; and Crittenden laughed.

"Git up an' shake hands, Jim," said Abe, sternly, to Crittenden's opponent, "an' let's have a drink." Reynolds got up slowly.

"You gimme a damn good lickin,'" he said to Crittenden. "Shake!"

Crittenden shook, and seconds and principals started for Long's tent.

"Boys," he said to the others, "I'm sorry fer ye. I ain't got but four drinks—and—" the old Sergeant was approaching; "and one more fer the Governor."

Rivers smiled broadly when he saw Crittenden at noon.

"The 'Governor' told me," he said, "you couldn't do anything in this regiment that would do you more good with officers and men. That fellow has caused us more trouble than any other ten men in the regiment, and you are the first man yet to get the best of him. If the men could elect you, you'd be a lieutenant before to-morrow night."

Crittenden laughed.

"It was disgusting, but I didn't see any other way out of it."

Tattoo was sounded.

"Are you sure you can get me into the army at any time?"

"Easy—as a private."

"What regiment?"

"Rough Riders or Regulars."

"All right, then, I'll go to Kentucky for you."

"No, old man. I was selfish enough to think it, but I'm not selfish enough to do it. I won't have it."

"But I want to go back. If I can get ın at the last moment I should go back anyhow to-night."

"Really?"

"Really. Just see that you let me know in time."

Rivers grasped his hand.

"I'll do that."

Next morning rumours were flying. In a week, at least, they would sail. And still regiments rolled in, and that afternoon Crittenden saw the regiment come in for which Grafton had been waiting—a picturesque body of fighting men and, perhaps, the most typical American regiment formed since Jackson fought at New Orleans. At the head of it rode two men —one with a quiet mesmeric power that bred perfect trust at sight, the other with a kindling power of enthusiasm, and a passionate energy, mental, physical, emotional, that was tireless; each a man among men, and both together an ideal leader for the thousand Americans at their heels. Behind them rode the Rough Riders— dusty, travel-stained troopers, gathered from every State, every walk of labour and leisure, every social grade in the Union—day labourer and millionaire, clerk and clubman, college boys and athletes, Southern revenue officers and Northern policemen; but most of them West-

erners—Texan rangers, sheriffs, and despera-
does—the men-hunters and the men-hunted;
Indians; followers of all political faiths, all
creeds—Catholics, Protestants, Jews; but cow-
boys for the most part; daredevils, to be sure,
but good-natured, good-hearted, picturesque,
fearless. And Americans—all!

As the last troopers filed past, Crittenden
followed them with his eyes, and he saw a little
way off Blackford standing with folded arms on
the edge of a cloud of dust and looking after
them too, with his face set as though he were
buried deep in a thousand memories. He started
when Crittenden spoke to him, and the dark fire
of his eyes flashed.

"That's where I belong," he said, with a
wave of his hand after the retreating column.
"I don't know one of them, and I know them
all. I've gone to college with some; I've hunted,
fished, camped, drank, and gambled with the
others. I belong with them; and I'm going with
them if I can; I'm trying to get an exchange
now."

"Well, luck to you, and good-by," said Crittenden, holding out his hand. "I'm going
home to-night."

"But you're coming back?"

"Yes."

Blackford hesitated.

"Are you going to join this outfit?"—meaning his own regiment.

"I don't know; this or the Rough Riders."

"Well," Blackford seemed embarrassed, and his manner was almost respectful, "if we go together, what do you say to our going as 'bunkies'?"

"Sure!"

"Thank you."

The two men grasped hands.

"I hope you will come back."

"I'm sure to come back. Good-by."

"Good-by, sir."

The unconscious "sir" startled Crittenden. It was merely habit, of course, and the fact that Crittenden was not yet enlisted, but there was an unintended significance in the soldier's tone that made him wince. Blackford turned sharply away, flushing.

VIII

BACK in the Bluegrass, the earth was flashing
with dew, and the air was brilliant with a
steady light that on its way from the sun was
broken by hardly a cloud. The woodland was
alive with bird-wing and bird-song and, under
them, with the flash of metal and the joy of
breaking camp. The town was a mighty pedes-
tal for flag-staffs. Everywhere flags were shaken
out. Main Street, at a distance, looked like a
long lane of flowers in a great garden—all blowing in a wind. Under them, crowds were gathered—country people, negroes, and townfolk—
while the town band stood waiting at the gate of
the park. The Legion was making ready to
leave for Chickamauga, and the town had made
ready to speed its going.

Out of the shady woodland, and into the bright
sunlight, the young soldiers came—to the music
of stirring horn and drum—legs swinging rhyth-
mically, chins well set in, eyes to the front—
wheeling into the main street in perfect form—
their guns a moving forest of glinting steel—
colonel and staff superbly mounted—every heart
beating proudly against every blue blouse, and

sworn to give up its blood for the flag waving over them—the flag the fathers of many had so bitterly fought five and thirty years before. Down the street went the flash and glitter and steady tramp of the solid columns, through waving flags and handkerchiefs and mad cheers —cheers that arose before them, swelled away on either side and sank out of hearing behind them as they marched—through faces bravely smiling, when the eyes were full of tears; faces tense with love, anxiety, fear; faces sad with bitter memories of the old war. On the end of the first rank was the boy Basil, file-leader of his squad, swinging proudly, his handsome face serious and fixed, his eyes turning to right nor left—seeing not his mother, proud, white, tear-less; nor Crittenden, with a lump of love in his throat; nor even little Phyllis—her pride in her boy-soldier swept suddenly out of her aching heart, her eyes brimming, and her handkerchief at her mouth to keep bravely back the sob that surged at her lips. The station at last, and then cheers and kisses and sobs, and tears and cheers again, and a waving of hands and flags and handkerchiefs—a column of smoke puffing on and on toward the horizon—the vanishing perspective of a rear platform filled with jolly, reckless, waving, yelling soldiers, and the tragedy of the parting was over.

How every detail of earth and sky was seared deep into the memory of the women left behind that afternoon—as each drove slowly homeward: for God help the women in days of war! The very peace of heaven lay upon the earth. It sank from the low, moveless clouds in the windless sky to the sunlit trees in the windless woods, as still as the long shadows under them. It lay over the still seas of bluegrass—dappled in woodland, sun-lit in open pasture—resting on low hills like a soft cloud of bluish-gray, clinging closely to every line of every peaceful slope. Stillness everywhere. Still cattle browsing in the distance; sheep asleep in the far shade of a cliff, shadowing the still stream; even the song of birds distant, faint, restful. Peace everywhere, but little peace in the heart of the mother to whose lips was raised once more the self-same cup that she had drained so long ago. Peace everywhere but for Phyllis climbing the stairs to her own room and flinging herself upon her bed in a racking passion of tears. God help the women in the days of war! Peace from the dome of heaven to the heart of the earth, but a gnawing unrest for Judith, who walked very slowly down the gravelled walk and to the stiles, and sat looking over the quiet fields. Only in her eyes was the light not wholly of sadness, but a proud light of sacrifice and high resolve. Crittenden was coming that night. He was going for good now; he was coming to tell her good-by; and he must not go—to his death, maybe—without knowing what she had to tell him. It was not much—it was very little, in return for his life-long devotion—that she should at least tell him how she had wholly outgrown her girlish infatuation— she knew now that it was nothing else—for the one man who had stood in her life before him, and that now there was no other—lover or friend—for whom she had the genuine affection that she would always have for him. She would tell him frankly—she was a grown woman now —because she thought she owed that much to him—because, under the circumstances, she thought it was her duty; and he would not misunderstand her, even if he really did not have quite the old feeling for her. Then, recalling what he had said on the drive, she laughed softly. It was preposterous. She understood all that. He had acted that little part so many times in by-gone years! And she had always pretended to take him seriously, for she would have given him mortal offence had she not; and she was pretending to take him seriously now. And, anyhow, what could he misunderstand? There was nothing to misunderstand.

And so, during her drive home, she had

thought all the way of him and of herself since
both were children—of his love and his long
faithfulness, and of her—her—what? Yes—she
had been something of a coquette—she had—she
had; but men had bothered and worried her,
and, usually, she couldn't help acting as she had.
She was so sorry for them all that she had really
tried to like them all. She had succeeded but
once—and even that was a mistake. But she
remembered one thing: through it all—far back
as it all was—she had never trifled with Crittenden. Before him she had dropped foil and
mask and stood frankly face to face always.
There was something in him that had always
forced that. And he had loved her through it
all, and he had suffered—how much, it had
really never occurred to her until she thought of
a sudden that he must have been hurt as had
she—hurt more; for what had been only infatuation with her had been genuine passion in
him; and the months of her unhappiness scarcely
matched the years of his. There was none other
in her life now but him, and, somehow, she was
beginning to feel there never would be. If there
were only any way that she could make amends.

Never had she thought with such tenderness
of him. How strong and brave he was; how
high-minded and faithful. And he was good,
in spite of all that foolish talk about himself.

And all her life he had loved her, and he had suffered. She could see that he was still unhappy. If, then, there was no other, and was to be no other, and if, when he came back from the war—why not?

Why not?

She felt a sudden warmth in her cheeks, her lips parted, and as she turned from the sunset her eyes had all its deep tender light.

Dusk was falling, and already Raincrow and Crittenden were jogging along toward her at that hour—the last trip for either for many a day—the last for either in life, maybe—for Raincrow, too, like his master, was going to war—while Bob, at home, forbidden by his young captain to follow him to Chickamauga, trailed after Crittenden about the place with the appealing look of a dog—enraged now and then by the taunts of the sharp-tongued Molly, who had the little confidence in the courage of her fellows that marks her race.

Judith was waiting for him on the porch, and Crittenden saw her from afar.

She was dressed for the evening in pure white —delicate, filmy—showing her round white throat and round white wrists. Her eyes were soft and welcoming and full of light; her manner was playful to the point of coquetry; and in sharp contrast, now and then, her face was intense with thought. A faint, pink light was still diffused from the afterglow, and she took him down into her mother's garden, which was old-fashioned and had grass-walks running down through it—bordered with pink beds and hedges of rose-bushes. And they passed under a shadowed grape-arbour and past a dead locust-tree, which a vine had made into a green tower of waving tendrils, and from which came the fragrant breath of wild grape, and back again to the gate, where Judith reached down for an old-fashioned pink and pinned it in his button-hole, talking with low, friendly affection meanwhile, and turning backward the leaves of the past rapidly.

Did he remember this—and that—and that? Memories—memories—memories. Was there anything she had let go unforgotten? And then, as they approached the porch in answer to a summons to supper, brought out by a little negro girl, she said:

"You haven't told me what regiment you are going with."

"I don't know."

Judith's eyes brightened. "I'm so glad you have a commission."

"I have no commission."

Judith looked puzzled. "Why, your mother ——"

"Yes, but I gave it to Basil." And he ex-

103

plained in detail. He had asked General Carter to give the commission to Basil, and the General had said he would gladly. And that morning the Colonel of the Legion had promised to recommend Basil for the exchange. This was one reason why he had come back to the Bluegrass. Judith's face was growing more thoughtful while he spoke, and a proud light was rising in her eyes.

"And you are going as——"

"As a private."

"With the Rough Riders?"

"As a regular—a plain, common soldier, with plain, common soldiers. I am trying to be an American now—not a Southerner. I've been drilling at Tampa and Chickamauga with the regulars."

"You are much interested?"

"More than in anything for years."

She had seen this, and she resented it, foolishly, she knew, and without reason—but, still, she resented it.

"Think of it," Crittenden went on. "It is the first time in my life, almost, I have known what it was to wish to do something—to have a purpose—that was not inspired by you." It was an unconscious and rather ungracious declaration of independence—it was unnecessary—and Judith was surprised, chilled—hurt.

104

"When do you go?"

Crittenden pulled a telegram from his pocket.

"To-morrow morning. I got this just as I was leaving town."

"To-morrow!"

"It means life or death to me—this telegram. And if it doesn't mean life, I don't care for the other. I shall come out with a commission or—not at all. If dead, I shall be a hero—if alive," he smiled, "I don't know what I'll be, but think of me as a hero, dead or alive, with my past and my present. I can feel a change already, a sort of growing pain, at the very thought."

"When do you go to Cuba?"

"Within four days."

"Four days! And you can talk as you do, when you are going to war to live the life of a common soldier—to die of fever, to be killed, maybe," her lip shook and she stopped, but she went on thickly, "and be thrown into an unknown grave or lie unburied in a jungle." She spoke with such sudden passion that Crittenden was startled.

"Listen!"

Judge Page appeared in the doorway, welcoming Crittenden with old-time grace and courtesy. Through supper, Judith was silent and thoughtful and, when she did talk, it was with a perceptible effort. There was a light in

her eyes that he would have understood once—
that would have put his heart on fire. And once
he met a look that he was wholly at loss to understand. After supper, she disappeared while the
two men smoked on the porch. The moon was
rising when she came out again. The breath of
honeysuckles was heavy on the air, and from
garden and fields floated innumerable odours of
flower and clover blossom and moist grasses.
Crittenden lived often through that scene afterward—Judith on the highest step of the porch,
the light from the hallway on her dress and her
tightly folded hands; her face back in shadow,
from which her eyes glowed with a fire in them
that he had never seen before.

Judge Page rose soon to go indoors. He did
not believe there was going to be much of a war,
and his manner was almost cheery when he bade
the young man good-by.

"Good luck to you," he said. "If the chance
comes, you will give a good account of yourself.
I never knew a man of your name who didn't."

"Thank you, sir."

There was a long silence.

"Basil will hardly have time to get his commission, and get to Tampa."

"No. But he can come after us."

She turned suddenly upon him.

"Yes—something has happened to you. I

didn't know what you meant that day we drove
home, but I do now. I feel it, but I don't
understand."

Crittenden flushed, but made no answer.

"You could not have spoken to me in the old
days as you do now. Your instinct would have
held you back. And something has happened
to me." Then she began talking to him as
frankly and simply as a child to a child. It was
foolish and selfish, but it had hurt her when he
told her that he no longer had his old feeling for
her. It was selfish and cruel, but it was true,
however selfish and cruel it seemed, and was—
but she had felt hurt. Perhaps that was vanity,
which was not to her credit—but that, too, she
could not help. It had hurt her every time he
had said anything from which she could infer
that her influence over him was less than it once
was—although, as a rule, she did not like to
have influence over people. Maybe he wounded
her as his friend in this way, and perhaps there
was a little vanity in this, too—but a curious
change was taking place in their relations. Once
he was always trying to please her, and in those
days she would have made him suffer if he had
spoken to her then as he had lately—but he
would not have spoken that way then. And now
she wondered why she was not angry instead of
being hurt. And she wondered why she did not

like him less. Somehow, it seemed quite fair that she should be the one to suffer now, and she was glad to take her share—she had caused him and others so much pain.

"*He*"—not even now did she mention his name—"wrote to me again, not long ago, asking to see me again. It was impossible. And it was the thought of you that made me know how impossible it was—*you*." The girl laughed, almost hardly, but she was thinking of herself when she did—not of him.

The time and circumstance that make woman the thing apart in a man's life must come sooner or later to all women, and women must yield; she knew that, but she had never thought they could come to her—but they had come, and she, too, must give way.

"It is all very strange," she said, as though she were talking to herself, and she rose and walked into the warm, fragrant night, and down the path to the stiles, Crittenden silently following. The night was breathless and the moon-lit woods had the still beauty of a dream; and Judith went on speaking of herself as she had never done—of the man whose name she had never mentioned, and whose name Crittenden had never asked. Until that night, he had not known even whether the man were still alive or dead. She had thought that was love—until lately she had never questioned but that when that was gone from her heart, all was gone that would ever be possible for her to know. That was why she had told Crittenden to conquer his love for her. And now she was beginning to doubt and to wonder—ever since she came back and heard him at the old auditorium—and why and whence the change now? That puzzled her. One thing was curious—through it all, as far back as she could remember, her feeling for him had never changed, except lately. Perhaps it was an unconscious response in her to the nobler change that in spite of his new hardness her instinct told her was at work in him.

She was leaning on the fence now, her elbow on the top plank, her hand under her chin, and her face uplifted—the moon lighting her hair, her face, and eyes, and her voice the voice of one slowly threading the mazes of a half-forgotten dream. Crittenden's own face grew tense as he watched her. There was a tone in her voice that he had hungered for all his life; that he had never heard but in his imaginings and in his dreams; that he had heard sounding in the ears of another and sounding at the same time the death-knell of the one hope that until now had made effort worth while. All evening she had played about his spirit as a wistful, changeful light will play over the fields when the moon is bright and clouds run swiftly. She turned on him like a flame now.

"Until lately," she was saying, and she was not saying at all what she meant to say; but here lately a change was taking place; something had come into her feeling for him that was new and strange—she could not understand—perhaps it had always been there; perhaps she was merely becoming conscious of it. And when she thought, as she had been thinking all day, of his long years of devotion—how badly she had requited them—it seemed that the least she could do was to tell him that he was now first in her life of all men—that much she could say; and perhaps he had always been, she did not know; perhaps, now that the half-gods were gone, it was at last the coming of the—the— She was deeply agitated now; her voice was trembling; she faltered, and she turned suddenly, sharply, and with a little catch in her breath, her lips and eyes opening slowly—her first consciousness, perhaps, a wonder at his strange silence—and dazed by her own feeling and flushing painfully, she looked at him for the first time since she began to talk, and she saw him staring fixedly at her with a half-agonized look, as though he were speechlessly trying to stop her, his face white, bitter, shamed, helpless.

Not a word more dropped from her lips—not a sound. She moved; it seemed that she was about to fall, and Crittenden started toward her, but she drew herself erect, and, as she turned—lifting her head proudly—the moonlight showed that her throat was drawn—nothing more. Motionless and speechless, Crittenden watched her white shape move slowly and quietly up the walk and grow dim; heard her light, even step on the gravel, up the steps, across the porch, and through the doorway. Not once did she look around.

.   .   .   .

He was in his room now and at his window, his face hard as stone when his heart was parching for tears. It was true, then. He was the brute he feared he was. He had killed his life, and he had killed his love—beyond even her power to recall. His soul, too, must be dead, and it were just as well that his body die. And, still bitter, still shamed and hopeless, he stretched out his arms to the South with a fierce longing for the quick fate—no matter what—that was waiting for him there.

IX

BY and by bulletins began to come in to the mother at Canewood from her boy at Tampa. There was little psychology in Basil's bulletin:

"I got here all right. My commission hasn't come, and I've joined the Rough Riders, for fear it won't get here in time. The Colonel was very kind to me—called me Mister.

"I've got a lieutenant's uniform of khaki, but I'm keeping it out of sight. I may have no use for it. I've got two left spurs, and I'm writing in the Waldorf-Astoria. I like these Northern fellows; they are gentlemen and plucky—I can see that. Very few of them swear. I wish I knew where brother is. The Colonel calls everybody Mister—even the Indians.

"Word comes to-night that we are to be off to the front. Please send me a piece of cotton to clean my gun. And please be easy about me —do be easy. And if you insist on giving

me a title, don't call me Private—call me
Trooper.

"Yes, we are going; the thing is serious. We
are all packed up now; have rolled up camping
outfit and are ready to start.

"Baggage on the transport now, and we sail
this afternoon. Am sorry to leave all of you,
and I have a tear in my eye now that I can't
keep back. It isn't a summer picnic, and I
don't feel like shouting when I think of home;
but I'm always lucky, and I'll come out all
right. I'm afraid I sha'n't see brother at all.
I tried to look cheerful for my picture (enclosed).
Good-by.

"Some delay; actually on board and steam
up.

"Waiting—waiting—waiting. It's bad enough
to go to Cuba in boats like these, but to
lie around for days is trying. No one goes
ashore, and I can hear nothing of brother. I
wonder why the General didn't give him that
commission instead of me. There is a curious
sort of fellow here, who says he knows brother.
His name is Blackford, and he is very kind to
me. He used to be a regular, and he says he
thinks brother took his place in the —th and is
a regular now himself—a private; I don't understand. There is mighty little Rough Riding
about this.

"P. S.—My bunkie is from Boston—Bob Sumner. His father *commanded a negro regiment in a fight once against my father;* think of it!

"Hurrah! we're off."

It was a tropical holiday—that sail down to Cuba—a strange, huge pleasure-trip of steamships, sailing in a lordly column of three; at night, sailing always, it seemed, in a harbour of brilliant lights under multitudinous stars and over thickly sown beds of tiny phosphorescent stars that were blown about like flowers in a wind-storm by the frothing wake of the ships; by day, through a brilliant sunlit sea, a cool breeze—so cool that only at noon was the heat tropical—and over smooth water, blue as sapphire. Music night and morning, on each ship, and music coming across the little waves at any hour from the ships about. Porpoises frisking at the bows and chasing each other in a circle around bow and stern as though the transports sat motionless; schools of flying-fish with filmy, rainbow wings rising from one wave and shimmering through the sunlight to the foamy crest of another—sometimes hundreds of yards away. Beautiful clear sunsets of rose, gold-green, and crimson, with one big, pure radiant star ever like a censor over them; every

114

night the stars more deeply and thickly sown and growing ever softer and more brilliant as the boats neared the tropics; every day dawn rich with beauty and richer for the dewy memories of the dawns that were left behind.

Now and then a little torpedo-boat would cut like a knife-blade through the water on messenger service; or a gunboat would drop lightly down the hill of the sea, along the top of which it patrolled so vigilantly; and ever on the horizon hung a battle-ship that looked like a great gray floating cathedral. But nobody was looking for a fight—nobody thought the Spaniard would fight—and so these were only symbols of war; and even they seemed merely playing the game.

It was as Grafton said. Far ahead went the flag-ship with the huge Commander-in-Chief and his staff, the gorgeous attachés, and the artists and correspondents, with valets, orderlies, stenographers, and secretaries. Somewhere, far to the rear, one ship was filled with newspaper men from stem to stern. But wily Grafton was with Lawton and Chaffee, the only correspondent aboard their transport. On the second day, as he sat on the poop-deck, a negro boy came up to him, grinning uneasily:

"I seed you back in ole Kentuck, suh."

"You did? Well, I don't remember seeing you. What do you want?"

"Captain say he gwine to throw me overboard."

"What for?"

"I ain't got no business here, suh."

"Then what are you here for?"

"Lookin' fer Ole Cap'n, suh."

"Ole Cap'n who?" said Grafton, mimicking.

"Cap'n Crittenden, suh."

"Well, if you are his servant, I suppose they won't throw you overboard. What's your name?"

"Bob, suh—Bob Crittenden."

"Crittenden," repeated Grafton, smiling. "Oh, yes, I know him; I should say so! So he's a Captain?"

"Yes, suh," said Bob, not quite sure whether he was lying or not.

Grafton spoke to an officer, and was allowed to take Bob for his own servant, though the officer said he did not remember any captain of that name in the —th. To the newspaper man, Bob was a godsend; for humour was scarce on board, and "jollying" Bob was a welcome diversion. He learned many things of Crittenden and the Crittendens, and what great people they had always been and still were; but at a certain point Bob was evasive or dumb —and the correspondent respected the servant's delicacy about family affairs and went no further along that line—he had no curiosity, and was questioning idly and for fun, but treated Bob kindly and, in return, the fat of the ship, through Bob's keen eye and quick hand, was his, thereafter, from day to day.

Grafton was not storing up much material for use; but he would have been much surprised if he could have looked straight across to the deck of the ship running parallel to his and have seen the dignified young statesman whom he had heard speak at the recruiting camp in Kentucky; who made him think of Henry Clay; whom he had seen whisking a beautiful girl from the camp in the smartest turn-out he had seen South—had seen him now as Private Crittenden, with his fast friend, Abe Long, and passing in his company because of his bearing under a soubriquet donated by his late enemy, Reynolds, as "Old Hamlet of Kentuck." And Crittenden would have been surprised had he known that the active darky whom he saw carrying coffee and shoes to a certain stateroom was none other than Bob waiting on Grafton. And that the Rough Rider whom he saw scribbling on a pad in the rigging of the *Yucatan* was none other than Basil writing one of his bulletins home.

It was hard for him to believe that he really was going to war, even now, when the long sail

was near an end and the ships were running
fearlessly along the big, grim coast-mountains
of Cuba, with bands playing and colors to the
breeze; hard to realize that he was not to land
in peace and safety and, in peace and safety, go
back as he came; that a little further down those
gashed mountains, showing ever clearer through
the mist, were men with whom the quiet officers
and men around him would soon be in a death-
grapple. The thought stirred him, and he
looked around at the big, strong fellows—intelligent, orderly, obedient, good-natured, and
patient; patient, restless, and sick as they were
from the dreadful hencoop life they had led for
so many days—patient beyond words. He had
risen early that morning. The rose light over
the eastern water was whitening, and all over the
deck his comrades lay asleep, their faces gray
in the coming dawn and their attitudes suggest-
ing ghastly premonitions—premonitions that
would come true fast enough for some of the
poor fellows—perhaps for him. Stepping between and over the prostrate bodies, he made
his way forward and leaned over the prow, with
his hat in his hand and his hair blowing back
from his forehead.

Already his face had suffered a change. For
more than three long weeks he had been merely
a plain man among plain men. At once when he

became Private Crittenden, No. 63, Company C, —th United States Regular Cavalry, at Tampa, he was shorn of his former estate as completely as though in the process he had been wholly merged into some other man. The officers, at whose table he had once sat, answered his salute precisely as they answered any soldier's. He had seen Rivers but seldom—but once only on the old footing, and that was on the night he went on board, when Rivers came to tell him good-by and to bitterly bemoan the luck that, as was his fear from the beginning, had put him among the ill-starred ones chosen to stay behind at Tampa and take care of the horses; as hostlers, he said, with deep disgust, adding hungrily:

"I wish I were in your place."

With the men, Crittenden was popular, for he did his work thoroughly, asked no favors, shirked no duties. There were several officers' sons among them working for commissions, and, naturally, he drifted to them, and he found them all good fellows. Of Blackford, he was rather wary, after Rivers's short history of him, but as he was friendly, unselfish, had a high sense of personal honour, and a peculiar reverence for women, Crittenden asked no further questions, and was sorry, when he came back to Tampa, to find him gone with the Rough Riders. With

Reynolds, he was particularly popular, and he never knew that the story of the Tampa fight had gone to all the line officers of the regiment, and that nearly every one of them knew him by sight and knew his history. Only once from an officer, however, and steadily always from the old Sergeant, could he feel that he was regarded in a different light from the humblest soldier in the ranks—which is just what he would have asked. The Colonel had cast an envious eye on Raincrow at Tampa, and, straightway, he had taken the liberty of getting the Sergeant to take the horse to the Colonel's tent with the request that he use him throughout the campaign. The horse came back with the Colonel's thanks; but, when the order came that the cavalry was to go unmounted, the Colonel sent word that he would take the horse now, as the soldier could not use him. So Raincrow was aboard the ship, and the old Colonel, coming down to look at the horse one day, found Crittenden feeding him, and thanked him and asked him how he was getting along; and, while there was a smile about his humorous mouth, there was a kindly look in his blue eyes that pleased Crittenden mightily. As for the old Sergeant, he could never forget that the soldier was a Crittenden—one of his revered Crittendens. And, while he was particularly stern with him in the presence of his comrades, for fear that he might be betrayed into showing partiality— he was always drifting around to give him a word of advice and to shake his head over the step that Crittenden had taken.

That step had made him good in body and soul. It made him lean and tanned; it sharpened and strengthened his profile; it cleared his eye and settled his lips even more firmly. Tobacco and liquor were scarce, and from disuse he got a new sensation of mental clearness and physical cleanliness that was comforting and invigorating, and helped bring back the freshness of his boyhood.

For the first time in many years, his days were full of work and, asleep, awake, or at work, his hours were clock-like and steadied him into machine-like regularity. It was work of his hands, to be sure, and not even high work of that kind, but still it was work. And the measure of the self-respect that this fact alone brought him was worth it all. Already, his mind was taking character from his body. He was distinctly less morbid and he found himself thinking during those long days of the sail of what he should do after the war was over. His desire to get killed was gone, and it was slowly being forced on him that he had been priggish, pompous, self-absorbed, hair-splitting, lazy, good-for-nothing, when there was no need for him to be other than what he meant to be when he got back. And as for Judith, he felt the bitterness of gall for himself when he thought of her, and he never allowed himself to think of her except to absolve her, as he knew she would not absolve herself, and to curse himself heartily and bitterly. He understood now. It was just her thought of his faithfulness, her feeling of responsibility for him—the thought that she had not been as kind to him as she might have been (and she had always been kinder than he deserved)—all this had loosed her tears and her self-control, and had thrown her into a mood of reckless self-sacrifice. And when she looked up into his face that night of the parting, he felt her looking into his soul and seeing his shame that he had lost his love because he had lost himself, and she was quite right to turn from him, as she did, without another word. Already, however, he was healthy enough to believe that he was not quite so hopeless as she must think him —not as hopeless as he had thought himself. Life, now, with even a soldier's work, was far from being as worthless as life with a gentleman's idleness had been. He was honest enough to take no credit for the clean change in his life—no other life was possible; but he was learning the practical value and mental comfort of straight living as he had never learned them before. And he was not so prone to metaphysics and morbid self-examination as he once was, and he shook off a mood of that kind when it came—impatiently—as he shook it off now. He was a soldier now, and his province was action and no more thought than his superiors allowed him. And, standing thus, at sunrise, on the plunging bow of the ship, with his eager, sensitive face splitting the swift wind—he might have stood to any thoughtful American who knew his character and his history as a national hope and a national danger. The nation, measured by its swift leap into maturity, its striking power to keep going at the same swift pace, was about his age. South, North, and West it had lived, or was living, his life. It had his faults and his virtues; like him, it was high-spirited, high-minded, alert, active, manly, generous, and with it, as with him, the bad was circumstantial, trivial, incipient; the good was bred in the Saxon bone and lasting as rock—if the surface evil were only checked in time and held down. Like him, it needed, like a Titan, to get back, now and then, to the earth to renew its strength. And the war would send the nation to the earth as it would send him, if he but lived it through.

There was little perceptible change in the

American officer and soldier, now that the work
was about actually to begin. A little more
soberness was apparent. Everyone was still
simple, natural, matter-of-fact. But that night,
doubtless, each man dreamed his dream. The
West Point stripling saw in his empty shoulder-
straps a single bar, as the man above him saw
two tiny bars where he had been so proud of
one. The Captain led a battalion, the Major
charged at the head of a thousand strong; the
Colonel plucked a star, and the Brigadier heard
the tramp of hosts behind him. And who knows
how many bold spirits leaped at once that night
from acorns to stars; and if there was not more
than one who saw himself the war-god of the
anxious nation behind—saw, maybe, even the
doors of the White House swing open at the con-
quering sound of his coming feet. And, through
the dreams of all, waved aimlessly the mighty
wand of the blind master—Fate—giving death
to a passion for glory here; disappointment bitter as death to a noble ambition there; and there
giving unsought fame where was indifference to
death; and then, to lend substance to the phantom of just deserts, giving a mortal here and
there the exact fulfilment of his dream.

Two toasts were drunk that night—one by
the men who were to lead the Rough Riders of
the West.

"May the war last till each man meets death, wears a wound, or wins himself better spurs."

And, in the hold of the same ship, another in whiskey from a tin cup between two comrades:

"Bunkie," said Blackford, to a dare-devil like himself, "welcome to the Spanish bullet that knocks for entrance here"—tapping his heart. Basil struck the cup from his hand, and Blackford swore, laughed, and put his arm around the boy.

X

ALREADY now, the first little fight was going on, and Grafton, the last newspaper man ashore, was making for the front—with Bob close at his heels. It was hot, very hot, but the road was a good, hard path of clean sand, and now and then a breeze stirred, or a light, cool rain twinkled in the air. On each side lay marsh, swamp, pool, and tropical jungle—and, to Grafton's Northern imagination, strange diseases lurked like monsters everywhere. Every strange, hot odour made him uneasy and, at times, he found himself turning his head and holding his breath, as he always did when he passed a pest-house in his childhood. About him were strange plants, strange flowers, strange trees, the music of strange birds, with nothing to see that was familiar except sky, mountain, running water, and sand; nothing home-like to hear but the twitter of swallows and the whistle of quail.

That path was no road for a hard-drinking man to travel and, now and then, Grafton shrank back, with a startled laugh, from the hideous things crawling across the road and rustling into the cactus—spiders with snail-houses over them; lizards with green bodies and yellow legs, and green legs and yellow bodies; hairy tarantulas, scorpions, and hideous mottled land-crabs, standing three inches from the sand, and watching him with hideous little eyes as they shuffled sidewise into the bushes. Moreover, he was following the trail of an army by the uncheerful signs in its wake—the *débris* of the last night's camp—empty cans, bits of hard-tack, crackers, bad odours, and, by and by, odds and ends that the soldiers discarded as the sun got warm and their packs heavy—drawers, undershirts, coats, blankets, knap-sacks, an occasional gauntlet or legging, bits of fat bacon, canned meats, hardtack—and a swarm of buzzards in the path, in the trees, and wheeling in the air—and smiling Cubans pick-ing up everything they could eat or wear.

An hour later, he met a soldier, who told him there had been a fight, Still, an hour later, rumours came thick, but so conflicting and wild that Grafton began to hope there had been no fight at all. Proof met him, then, in the road—a white man, on foot, with his arm in a bloody sling. Then, on a litter, a negro trooper with a shattered leg; then another with a bullet through his throat; and another wounded man, and another. On horseback rode a Sergeant with a bandage around his brow—Grafton could see him smiling broadly fifty yards ahead—and the furrow of a Mauser bullet across his temple, and just under his skin.

"Still nutty," said Grafton to himself.

Further on was a camp of insurgents—little, thin, brown fellows, ragged, dirty, shoeless— each with a sugar-loaf straw hat, a Remington rifle of the pattern of 1882, or a brand new Krag-Jorgensen donated by Uncle Sam, and the inevitable and ever ready machete swinging in a case of embossed leather on the left hip. Very young they were, and very old; and wiry, quick-eyed, intelligent, for the most part and, in countenance, vivacious and rather gentle. There was a little creek next, and, climbing the bank of the other side, Grafton stopped short, with a start, in the road. To the right and on a sloping bank lay eight gray shapes, muffled from head to foot, and Grafton would have known that all of them were in their last sleep, but one, who lay with his left knee bent and upright, his left elbow thrust from his blanket, and his hand on his heart. He slept like a child.

Beyond was the camp of the regulars who had taken part in the fight. On one side stood a Colonel, who himself had aimed a Hotchkiss gun in the last battle—covered with grime and sweat, and with the passion of battle not quite gone from his eyes; and across the road soldiers were digging one long grave. Grafton pushed on a little further, and on the top of the ridge and on the grassy sun-lit knoll was the camp of the Riders, just beyond the rifle-pits from which they had driven the Spaniards. Under a tree to the right lay another row of muffled shapes, and at once Grafton walked with the Colonel to the hospital, a quarter of a mile away. The path, thickly shaded and dappled with sunshine, ran along the ridge through the battle-field, and it was as pretty, peaceful, and romantic as a lovers' walk in a garden. Here and there, the tall grass along the path was pressed flat where a wounded man had lain. In one place, the grass was matted and dark red; nearby was a blood-stained hat marked with the initials "E. L." Here was the spot where the first victim of the fight fell. A passing soldier, who reluctantly gave his name as Blackford, bared his left arm and showed the newspaper man three places between his wrist and elbow where the skin had been merely blistered by three separate bullets as he lay fighting unseen enemies. Further on, lay a dead Spaniard, with covered face.

"There's one," said the Colonel, with a careless gesture. A huge buzzard flapped from the tree over the dead man as they passed beneath.

Beyond was the open-air hospital, where two more rigid human figures, and where the wounded lay—white, quiet, uncomplaining.

And there a surgeon told him how the wounded had lain there during the fight singing:

" My Country, 'tis of thee! "

And Grafton beat his hands together, while his throat was full and his eyes were full of tears. To think what he had missed—to think what he had missed!

He knew that national interest would centre in this regiment of Rough Riders; for every State in the Union had a son in its ranks, and the sons represented every social element in the national life. Never was there a more representative body of men, nor a body of more varied elements standing all on one and the same basis of American manhood. He recalled how, at Tampa, he had stood with the Colonel while the regiment filed past, the Colonel, meanwhile, telling him about the men—the strong men, who made strong stories for Wister and strong pictures for Remington. And the Colonel had pointed with especial pride and affection to two boy troopers, who marched at the head of his column—a Puritan from Massachusetts and a Cavalier through Virginia blood from Kentucky; one the son of a Confederate General, the other the son of a Union General—both beardless "bunkies," brothers in arms, and fast becoming brothers at heart—Robert Sumner and Basil Crittenden. The Colonel waved his hand toward the wild Westerners who followed them.

"It's odd to think it—but those two boys are the fathers of the regiment."

And now that Grafton looked around and thought of it again—they were. The fathers of the regiment had planted Plymouth and Jamestown; had wrenched life and liberty and civilization from the granite of New England, the fastnesses of the Cumberland, and the wildernesses of the rich valleys beyond; while the sires of these very Westerners had gone on with the same trinity through the barren wastes of plains. And, now, having conquered the New World, Puritan and Cavalier, and the children of both were come together again on the same old mission of freedom, but this time the freedom of others; carrying the fruits of their own struggle back to the old land from which they came, with the sword in one hand, if there was need, but with the torch of liberty in the other—held high, and, as God's finger pointed, lighting the way.

To think what he had missed!

As Grafton walked slowly back, an officer

was calling the roll of his company under the
quiet, sunny hill, and he stopped to listen.
Now and then there was no answer, and he
went on—thrilled and saddened. The play was
ended—this was war.

Outside the camp the road was full of half-
angry, bitterly disappointed infantry—Chaffee's
men. When he reached the camp of the cavalry
at the foot of the hill again, a soldier called his
name as he passed—a grimy soldier—and Grafton stopped in his tracks.

"Well, by God!"

It was Crittenden, who smiled when he saw
Grafton's bewildered face. Then the Kentuckian, too, stared in utter amazement at a
black face grinning over Grafton's shoulder.

"Bob!" he said, sharply.

"Yessuh," said Bob humbly.

"Whar are you doing here?"

"Nothin', Ole Cap'n—jes doin' nothin'," said
Bob, with the _naïveté_ of a child. "Jes lookin'
for you."

"Is that your negro?" A sarcastic Lieutenant was asking the question.

"He's my servant, sir."

"Well, we don't allow soldiers to take their
valets to the field."

"My servant at home, sir, I meant. He
came of his own accord."

"Nothin', Ole Cap'n—jes doin' nothin'—jes lookin' for you."

"Go find Basil," Crittenden said to Bob, "and if you can't find him," he added in a lower tone, "and want anything, come back here to me."

"Yessuh," said Bob, loath to go, but, seeing the Lieutenant scowling, he moved on down the road.

"I thought you were a Captain," said Grafton. Crittenden laughed.

"Not exactly."

"Forward," shouted the Lieutenant, "march!"

Grafton looked Crittenden over.

"Well, I swear," he said heartily, and, as Crittenden moved forward, Grafton stood looking after him. "A regular—I do be damned!"

That night Basil wrote home. He had not fired his musket a single time. He saw nothing to shoot at, and he saw no use shooting until he did have something to shoot at. It was terrible to see men dead and wounded, but the fight itself was stupid—blundering through a jungle, bullets zipping about, and the Spaniards too far away and invisible. He wanted to be closer.

"General Carter has sent for me to take my place on his staff. I don't want to go, but the Colonel says I ought. I don't believe I would, if the General hadn't been father's friend and if my 'bunkie' weren't wounded. He's all right, but he'll have to go back. I'd like to have his wound, but I'd hate to have to go back. The Colonel says he's sorry to lose me. He meant to make me a corporal, he says. I don't know what for—but Hooray!

"Brother was not in the fight, I suppose. Don't worry about me—please don't worry.

"P. S.—I have often wondered what it would be like to be on the eve of a battle. It's no different from anything else."

Abe Long and Crittenden were bunkies now. Abe's comrade, the boy Sanders, had been wounded and sent to the rear. Reynolds, too, was shot through the shoulder, and, despite his protests, was ordered back to the coast.

"Oh, I'll be on hand for the next scrap," he said.

Abe and Crittenden had been side by side in the fight. It was no surprise to Crittenden that any man was brave. By his code, a man would be better dead than alive a coward. He believed cowardice exceptional and the brave man the rule, but he was not prepared for Abe's coolness and his humour. Never did the Westerner's voice change, and never did the grim half-smile leave his eyes or his mouth. Once during the fight he took off his hat.

"How's my hair parted?" he asked, quietly. A Mauser bullet had mowed a path through Abe's thick, upright hair, scraping the skin for three inches, and leaving a trail of tiny, red drops. Crittenden turned to look and laugh, and a bullet cut through the open flap of his shirt, just over his heart. He pointed to it.

"See the good turn you did me."

While the two were cooking supper, the old Sergeant came up.

"If you don't obey orders next time," he said to Crittenden, sternly, for Abe was present, "I'll report you to the Captain." Crittenden had declined to take shelter during the fight— it was a racial inheritance that both the North and the South learned to correct in the old war.

"That's right, Governor," said Abe.

"The Colonel himself wanted to know what damn fool that was standing out in the road. He meant you."

"All right, Sergeant," Crittenden said.

When he came in from guard duty, late that night, he learned that Basil was safe. He lay down with a grateful heart, and his thoughts, like the thoughts of every man in that tropical forest, took flight for home. Life was getting very simple now for him—death, too, and duty. Already he was beginning to wonder at his old self and, with a shock, it came to him that there were but three women in the world to him— Phyllis and his mother—and Judith. He thought of the night of the parting, and it flashed for the first time upon him that Judith might have taken the shame that he felt reddening his face as shame for her, and not for himself: and a pain shot through him so keen that he groaned aloud.

Above him was a clear sky, a quarter moon, an enveloping mist of stars, and the very peace of heaven. But there was little sleep—and that battle-haunted—for any: and for him none at all.

.   .   .   .

And none at all during that night of agony for Judith, nor Phyllis, nor the mother at Canewood, though there was a reaction of joy, next morning, when the name of neither Crittenden was among the wounded or the dead.

Nothing had been heard, so far, of the elder brother but, as they sat in the porch, a negro boy brought the town paper, and Mrs. Crittenden found a paragraph about a soldier springing into the sea in full uniform at Siboney to rescue a drowning comrade, who had fallen into the surf while trying to land, and had been sunk to the bottom by his arms and ammunition. And the rescuer's name was Crittenden. The writer went on to tell who he was, and how he had given up his commission to a younger brother and had gone as a private in the regular army—how he had been offered another after he reached Cuba, and had declined that, too—having entered with his comrades, he would stay with them to the end. Whereat the mother's face burned with a proud fire, as did Phyllis's, when Mrs. Crittenden read on about this Crittenden's young brother, who, while waiting for his commission, had gone as a Rough Rider, and who, after gallant conduct during the first fight, had taken his place on General Carter's staff. Phyllis clapped her hands, softly, with a long sigh of pride—and relief.

"I can eat strawberries, now." And she blushed again. Phyllis had been living on bacon and corn-bread, she confessed shame-facedly, because Trooper Basil was living on bacon and hardtack—little dreaming that the food she forced upon herself in this sacrificial way was being swallowed by that hearty young-ster with a relish that he would not have known at home for fried chicken and hot rolls.

"Yes," laughed Mrs. Crittenden. "You can eat strawberries now. You can balance them against his cocoanuts."

Phyllis picked up the paper then, with a cry of surprise—the name signed to the article was Grafton, whom she had seen at the recruiting camp. And then she read the last paragraph that the mother had not read aloud, and she turned sharply away and stooped to a pink-bed, as though she would pick one, and the mother saw her shoulders shaking with silent sobs, and she took the child in her arms.

There was to be a decisive fight in a few days —the attack on Santiago—that was what Phyllis had read. The Spaniard had a good muster-roll of regulars and aid from Cervera's fleet; was well armed, and had plenty of time to in-trench and otherwise prepare himself for a bloody fight in the last ditch.

So that, each day there was a relief to the night agony, which, every morning, began straightway with the thought that the fight might be going on at that very hour. Not once did Judith come near. She had been ill, to be sure, but one day Mrs. Crittenden met her on the way to town and stopped her in the road; but the girl had spoken so strangely that the mother drove on, at loss to understand and much hurt. Next day she learned that Judith, despite her ill health and her father's protests, had gone to nurse the sick and the wounded— what Phyllis plead in vain to do. The following day a letter came from Mrs. Crittenden's elder son. He was well, and the mother must not worry about either him or Basil. He did not think there would be much fighting and, any-how, the great risk was from disease, and he feared very little ᶠrom that. Basil would be much safer as an aid on a General's staff. He would get plenty to eat, would be less exposed to weather, have no long marches—as he would be mounted—and no guard duty at all hours of day and night. And, moreover, he would probably be less constantly exposed to bullets. So she must not worry about him. Not one word was there about Judith—not even to ask how she was, which was strange. He had said nothing about the girl when he told his mother good-by; and when she broached the subject, he answered sadly:

"Don't, mother; I can't say a word—not a word."

In his letter he had outlined Basil's advantages, not one of which was his—and sitting on the porch of the old homestead at sunset of the last rich day in June, the mother was following her eldest born through the transport life, the fiery marches, the night watches on lonely outposts, the hard food, the drenching rains, steaming heat, laden with the breath of terrible disease, not realizing how little he minded it all and how much good it was doing him. She did know, however, that it had been but play thus far to what must follow. Perhaps, even now, she thought, the deadly work was beginning, while she sat in the shrine of peace—even now.

And it was. Almost at that hour the troops

were breaking camp and moving forward along the one narrow jungle-road—choked with wagon, pack-mule, and soldier—through a haze of dust, and, turning to the right at the first crossing beyond corps head-quarters—under Chaffee—for Caney. Now and then a piece of artillery, with its flashes of crimson, would pass through the advancing columns amid the waving of hats and a great cheering to take position against the stone fort at Caney or at El Poso, to be trained on the block-house at San Juan. And through the sunset and the dusk the columns marched, and, after night fell, the dark, silent masses of slouch hats, shoulders, and gun-muzzles kept on marching past the smoke and flare of the deserted camp-fires that lighted thicket and grassy plot along the trail. And after the flames had died down to cinders—in the same black terrible silence, the hosts were marching still.

That night a last good-by to all womankind, but wife, mother, sister, sweetheart. The world was to be a man's world next day, and the man a coarse, dirty, sweaty, swearing, good-natured, grimly humorous, cruel, kindly soldier, feverish for a fight and as primitive in passion as a cave-dweller fighting his kind for food. The great little fight was at hand.

XI

BEFORE dawn again—everything in war begins at dawn—and the thickets around a certain little gray stone fort alive with slouch hat, blue blouse, and Krag-Jorgensen, slipping through the brush, building no fires, and talking in low tones for fear the timorous enemy would see, or hear, and run before the American sharpshooter could get a chance to try his marksmanship; wondering, eight hours later, if the timorous enemy were ever going to run. Eastward and on a high knoll stripped of bushes, four 3.2 guns unlimbered and thrown into position against that fort and a certain little red-roofed town to the left of it. This was Caney.

Eastward still, three miles across an uneven expanse of green, jungle and jungle-road alive with men, bivouacing fearlessly around and under four more 3.2 guns planted on another high-stripped knoll—El Poso—and trained on a little pagoda-like block-house, which sat like a Christmas toy on top of a green little, steep little hill from the base of which curved an orchard-like valley back to sweeping curve of the jungle. This was San Juan.

Nature loves sudden effects in the tropics.
While Chaffee fretted in valley-shadows around
Caney and Lawton strode like a yellow lion past
the guns on the hill and, eastward, gunner on
the other hill at El Poso and soldier in the jungle
below listened westward, a red light ran like a
flame over the east, the tops of the mountains
shot suddenly upward and it was day—flashing
day, with dripping dew and birds singing and a
freshness of light and air that gave way suddenly
when the sun quickly pushed an arc of fire over
the green shoulder of a hill and smote the soldiers
over and under the low trees like rays from an
open furnace.

It smote Reynolds as he sat by the creek under
the guns before San Juan, idly watching water
bubble into three canteens, and it opened his
lips for an oath that he was too lazy to speak;
it smote Abe Long cooking coffee on the bank
some ten yards away, and made him raise from
the fire and draw first one long forearm and
then the other across his heat-wrinkled brow;
but, unheeded, it smote Crittenden—who stood
near, leaning against a palm-tree—full in his
uplifted face. Perhaps that was the last sunrise
on earth for him. He was watching it in Cuba,
but his spirit was hovering around home. He
could feel the air from the woods in front of
Canewood; could hear the darkies going to work

and Aunt Keziah singing in the kitchen. He could see his mother's shutter open, could see her a moment later, smiling at him from her door. And Judith—where was she, and what was she doing? Could she be thinking of him? The sound of his own name coming down through the hot air made him start, and, looking up toward the Rough Riders, who were gathered about a little stuccoed farm-house just behind the guns on the hill, he saw Blackford waving at him. At the same moment hoofs beat the dirt-road behind him—familiar hoof-beats— and he turned to see Basil and Raincrow—for Crittenden's Colonel was sick with fever and Basil had Raincrow now—on their way with a message to Chaffee at Caney. Crittenden saluted gravely, as did Basil, though the boy turned in his saddle, and with an affectionate smile waved back at him.

Crittenden's lips moved.

"God bless him."

. . . .

"Fire!"

Over on the hill, before Caney, a man with a lanyard gave a quick jerk. There was a cap explosion at the butt of the gun and a bulging white cloud from the muzzle; the trail bounced from its shallow trench, the wheels whirled back twice on the rebound, and the shell was hissing

through the air as iron hisses when a black-
smith thrusts it red-hot into cold water. Basil
could hear that awful hiss so plainly that he
seemed to be following the shell with his naked
eye; he could hear it above the reverberating
roar of the gun up and down the coast-mountain;
hear it until, six seconds later, a puff of smoke
answered beyond the Spanish column where the
shell burst. Then in eight seconds—for the shell
travelled that much faster than sound—the
muffled report of its bursting struck his ears,
and all that was left of the first shot that started
the great little fight was the thick, sunlit smoke
sweeping away from the muzzle of the gun and
the little mist-cloud of the shell rising slowly
upward beyond the stone fort, which seemed
not to know any harm was possible or near.

.   .   .   .

Again Crittenden, leaning against the palm,
heard his name called. Again it was Blackford
who was opening his mouth to shout some message when—Ah! The shout died on Blackford's
lips, and every man on the hill and in the woods,
at that instant, stayed his foot and his hand—
even a man standing with a gray horse against
the blue wall—he, too, stopped to listen. It
really sounded too dull and muffled for a shell;
but, a few seconds later, there was a roar against
the big walls of living green behind Caney.

The first shot!

"Ready!"

Even with the cry at El Poso came another sullen, low boom and another aggressive roar from Caney: then a great crackling in the air, as though thousands of school-boys were letting off fire-crackers, pack after pack.

"Fire!"

Every ear heard, every eye saw the sudden white mist at a gun-muzzle and followed that first shell screaming toward the little Christmas toy sitting in the sun on that distant little hill. And yet it was nothing. Another and yet another mass of shrapnel went screaming, and still there was no response, no sign. It was nothing—nothing at all. Was the Spaniard asleep?

Crittenden could see attaché, correspondent, aid, staff-officer, non-combatant, sight-seer crowding close about the guns—so close that the gunners could hardly work. He could almost hear them saying, one to another:

"Why, is this war—really war? Why, this isn't so bad."

Twanged just then a bow-string in the direction of San Juan hill, and the twang seemed to be getting louder and to be coming toward the little blue farm-house. No cannon was in sight; there was no smoke visible, and many, with an upward look, wondered what the queer sound

145

could be. Suddenly there was a screeching, crackling answer in the air; the atmosphere was rent apart as by a lightning stroke directly over-head. The man and the horse by the blue wall dropped noiselessly to the earth. A Rough Rider paled and limped down the hill and Black-ford shook his hand—a piece of shrapnel had fallen harmlessly on his wrist. On the hill—Crittenden laughed as he looked—on the hill, nobody ran—everybody tumbled. Besides the men at the guns, only two others were left—civilians.

"You're a fool," said one.

"You're another."

"What'd you stay here for?"

"Because you did. What'd you stay for?"

"Because *you* did."

Then they went down together—rapidly—and just in time. Another shell shrieked. Two artillerymen and two sergeants dropped dead at their guns, and a corporal fell, mortally wounded. A third burst in a group of Cubans. Several of them flew out, killed or wounded, into the air; the rest ran shrieking for the woods. Below, those woods began to move. Under those shells started the impatient soldiers down that narrow lane through the jungle, and with Reynolds and Abe Long on the "point" was Crittenden, his Krag-Jorgensen across his breast—thrilled, for all the world, as though he were on a hunt for big game.

. . . .

And all the time the sound of ripping cloth was rolling over from Caney, the far-away rumble of wagons over cobble-stones, or softened stage hail and stage thunder around the block-house, stone fort, and town. At first it was a desultory fire, like the popping of a bunch of fire-crackers that have to be relighted several times, and Basil and Grafton, galloping toward it, could hear the hiss of bullets that far away. But, now and then, the fire was as steady as a Gatling-gun. Behind them the artillery had turned on the stone fort, and Grafton saw one shot tear a hole through the wall, then another, and another. He could see Spaniards darting from the fort and taking refuge in the encircling stone-cut trenches; and then nothing else—for their powder was smokeless—except the straw hats of the little devils in blue, who blazed away from their trenches around the fort and minded the shells bursting over and around them as little as though they had been bursting snowballs. If the boy ahead noted anything, Grafton could not tell. Basil turned his head neither to right nor left, and at the foot of the muddy hill, the black horse that he rode, without touch of spur, seemed suddenly to leave the earth and pass on out of sight with the swift silence of a shadow. At the foot of a hill walked the first wounded man—a Colonel limping between two soldiers. The Colonel looked up smiling—he had a terrible wound in the groin.

"Well," he called cheerily, "I'm the first victim."

Grafton wondered. Was it possible that men were going to behave on a battle-field just as they did anywhere else—just as naturally—taking wounds and death and horror as a matter of course? Beyond were more wounded—the wounded who were able to help themselves. Soon he saw them lying by the roadside, here and there a dead one; by and by, he struck a battalion marching to storm a block-house. He got down, hitched his horse a few yards from the road and joined it. He was wondering how it would feel to be under fire, when just as they were crossing another road, with a whir and whistle and buzz, a cloud of swift insects buzzed over his head. Unconsciously imitating the soldiers near him, he bent low and walked rapidly. Right and left of him sounded two or three low, horrib e crunching noises, and right and left of him two or three blue shapes sank limply down on their faces. A sudden sickness seized him, nauseating him like a fetid odour—the crunching noise was the sound of a bullet crashing into

a living human skull as the men bent forward.
One man, he remembered afterward, dropped
with the quick grunt of an animal—he was
killed outright; another gave a gasping cry,
"Oh, God"—there was a moment of suffering
consciousness for him; a third hopped aside into
the bushes—cursing angrily. Still another, as
he passed, looked up from the earth at him with
a curious smile, as though he were half ashamed
of something.

"I've got it, partner," he said, "I reckon I've
got it, sure." And Grafton saw a drop of blood
and the tiny mouth of a wound in his gullet,
where the flaps of his collar fell apart. He
couldn't realize how he felt—he was not interested any longer in how he felt. The instinct of
life was at work, and the instinct of self-defence.
When the others dropped, he dropped gladly;
when they rose, he rose automatically. A piece
of brush, a bush, the low branch of a tree, a
weed seemed to him protection, and he saw
others possessed with the same absurd idea.
Once the unworthy thought crossed his mind,
when he was lying behind a squad of soldiers
and a little lower than they, that his chance was
at least better than theirs. And once, and only
once—with a bitter sting of shame—he caught
himself dropping back a little, so that the same
squad should be between him and the enemy:

and forthwith he stepped out into the road,
abreast with the foremost, cursing himself for a
coward, and thereafter took a savage delight in
reckless exposure whenever it was possible.
And he soon saw that his position was a queer
one, and an unenviable one, as far as a cool test
of nerve was the point at issue. The officers, he
saw, had their men to look after—orders to obey
—their minds were occupied. The soldiers were
busy getting a shot at the enemy—their minds,
too, were occupied. It was his peculiar province to stand up and be shot at without the
satisfaction of shooting back—studying his sen-
sations, meanwhile, which were not particularly
pleasant, and studying the grewsome horrors
about him. And it struck him, too, that this was
a ghastly business, and an unjustifiable, and
that if it pleased God to see him through he
would never go to another war except as a soldier. One consideration interested him and was
satisfactory. Nobody was shooting at him—
nobody was shooting at anybody in particular.
If he were killed, or when anybody was killed,
it was merely accident, and it was thus pleasant
to reflect that he was in as much danger as
anybody.

The firing was pretty hot now, and the wounded were too many to be handled. A hospital
man called out sharply:

"Give a hand here." Grafton gave a hand to help a poor fellow back to the field hospital, in a little hollow, and when he reached the road again that black horse and his boy rider were coming back like shadows, through a rain of bullets, along the edge of the woods. Once the horse plunged sidewise and shook his head angrily—a Mauser had stung him in the neck— but the lad, pale and his eyes like stars, lifted him in a flying leap over a barbed-wire fence and swung him into the road again.

"Damn!" said Grafton, simply.

Then rose a loud cheer from the battery on the hill, and, looking west, he saw the war-balloon hung high above the trees and moving toward Santiago. The advance had begun over there; there was the main attack—the big battle. It was interesting and horrible enough where he was, but Caney was not Santiago; and Grafton, too, mounted his horse and galloped after Basil.

.   .   .   .

At head-quarters began the central lane of death that led toward San Juan, and Basil picked his way through it at a slow walk—his excitement gone for the moment and his heart breaking at the sight of the terrible procession on its way to the rear. Men with arms in slings; men with trousers torn away at the knee, and bandaged legs; men with brow, face, mouth, or throat swathed; men with no shirts, but a broad swathe around the chest or stomach—each bandage grotesquely pictured with human figures printed to show how the wound should be bound, on whatever part of the body the bullet entered. Men staggering along unaided, or between two comrades, or borne on litters, some white and quiet, some groaning and blood-stained, some conscious, some dying, some using a rifle for a support, or a stick thrust through the side of a tomato-can. Rolls, haversacks, blouses, hardtack, bibles, strewn by the wayside, where the soldiers had thrown them before they went into action. It was curious, but nearly all of the wounded were dazed and drunken in appearance, except at the brows, which were tightly drawn with pain. There was one man, with short, thick, upright red hair, stumbling from one side of the road to the other, with no wound apparent, and muttering:

"Oh, I don't know what happened to me. I don't know what happened to me."

Another, hopping across the creek on one leg —the other bare and wounded—and using his gun, muzzle down, as a vaulting-pole. Another, with his arm in the sling, pointing out the way.

"Take this road," he said. "I don't know where that one goes, but I know this one. I went up this one, and brought back a *souvenir*," he added, cheerily, shaking a bloody arm.

And everywhere men were cautioning him to beware of the guerillas, who were in the trees, adding horror to the scene—shooting wounded men on litters, hospital men, doctors. Once, there was almost the horror of a panic in the crowded road. Soldiers answered the guerilla fire from the road; men came running back; bullets spattered around.

Ahead, the road was congested with soldiers. Beyond them was anchored the balloon, over the Bloody Ford—drawing the Spanish fire to the troops huddled beneath it. There was the death-trap.

And, climbing from an ambulance to mount his horse, a little, bent old man, weak and trembling from fever, but with his gentle blue eyes glinting fire—Basil's hero—ex-Confederate Jerry Carter.

"Give the Yanks hell, boys," he shouted.

.   .   .   .

It had been a slow, toilsome march up that narrow lane of death, and, so far, Crittenden had merely been sprinkled with Mauser and shrapnel. His regiment had begun to deploy to the left, down the bed of a stream. The negro cavalry and the Rough Riders were deploying to the right. Now broke the storm. Imagine sheet after sheet of hailstones, coated with polished steel, and swerved when close to the earth at a sharp angle to the line of descent, and sweeping the air horizontally with an awful hiss—swifter in flight than a peal of thunder from sky to earth, and hardly less swift than the lightning flash that caused it.

"T-t-seu-u-u-h! T-t-seu-oo! T-t-seu-oo!"— they went like cloud after cloud of lightning-winged insects, and passing, by God's mercy and the Spaniard's bad marksmanship—passing high. Between two crashes, came a sudden sputter, and some singing thing began to play up and down through the trees, and to right and left, in a steady hum. It was a machine gun playing for the range—like a mighty hose pipe, watering earth and trees with a steady, spreading jet of hot lead. It was like some strange, huge monster, unseeing and unseen, who knows where his prey is hidden and is searching for it blindly—by feeling or by sense of smell—coming ever nearer, showering the leaves down, patting into the soft earth ahead, swishing to right and to left, and at last playing in a steady stream about the prostrate soldiers.

"Swish-ee! Swish-ee! Swishee!"

"Whew!" said Abe Long.

"God!" said Reynolds.

Ah, ye scornful veterans of the great war.

In ten minutes the Spaniard let fly with his Mauser more bullets than did you fighting hard for two long hours, and that one machine gun loosed more death stings in an hour than did a regiment of you in two. And they were coming from intrenchments on an all but vertical hill, from piles of unlimited ammunition, and from soldiers who should have been as placid as the earth under them for all the demoralization that hostile artillery fire was causing them.

And not all of them passed high. After that sweep of glistening steel rain along the edge of the woods rose the cry here, there, everywhere:

"Hospital man! hospital man!"

And here and there, in the steady pelt of bullets, went the quiet, brave fellows with red crosses on their sleeves; across the creek, Crittenden could see a tall, young doctor, bareheaded in the sun, stretching out limp figures on the sand under the bank—could see him and his assistants stripping off blouse and trousers and shirt, and wrapping and binding, and newly wounded being ever brought in.

And behind forged soldiers forward, a tall aide at the ford urging them across and stopping a panic among volunteers.

"Come back, you cowards—come back! Push 'em back, boys!"

A horse was crossing the stream. There was

a hissing shriek in the air, a geyser spouting from the creek, the remnants of a horse thrown upward, and five men tossed in a swirl like straw: and, a moment later, a boy feebly paddling towards the shore—while the water ran past him red with blood. And, through it all, looking backward, Crittenden saw little Carter coming on horseback, calm of face, calm of manner, with his hands folded over his saddle, and his eyes looking upward—little Carter who had started out in an ambulance that morning with a temperature of one hundred and four, and, meeting wounded soldiers, gave up his wagon to them, mounted his horse, and rode into battle—to come out normal at dusk. And behind him—erect, proud, face aflame, eyes burning, but hardly less cool—rode Basil. Crittenden's eyes filled with love and pride for the boy.

"God bless him—God save him!"

. . . .

A lull came—one of the curious lulls that come periodically in battle for the reason that after any violent effort men must have a breathing spell—and the mist of bullets swept on to the right like a swift passing shower of rain.

There was a splash in the creek behind Crittenden, and someone fell on his face behind the low bank with a fervent:

"Thank God, I've got this far!" It was Grafton.

"That nigger of yours is coming on somewhere back there," he added, and presently he rose and calmly peered over the bank and at the line of yellow dirt on the crest of the hill. A bullet spat in the ground close by.

"That hit you?" he asked, without altering the tone of his voice—without even lowering his glasses.

Reynolds, on his right, had ducked quickly. Crittenden looked up in surprise. The South had no monopoly of nerve—nor, in that campaign, the soldier.

"Well, by God," said Reynolds, irritably— the bullet had gone through his sleeve. "This ain't no time to joke."

Grafton's face was still calm—he was still looking. Presently he turned and beckoned to somebody in the rear.

"There he is, now."

Looking behind, Crittenden had to laugh. There was Bob, in a cavalryman's hat, with a Krag-Jorgensen in his hand, and an ammunition belt buckled around him.

As he started toward Grafton, a Lieutenant halted him.

"Why aren't you with your regiment?" he demanded sharply.

"I ain't got no regiment. I'se looking fer Ole Captain."

"Get back into your regiment," said the officer, with an oath, and pointing behind to the Tenth Coloured Cavalry coming up.

"Huh!" he said, looking after the officer a moment, and then he came on to the edge of the creek.

"Go to the rear, Bob," shouted Crittenden, sharply, and the next moment Bob was crashing through the bushes to the edge of the creek.

"Foh Gawd, Ole Cap'n, I sutn'ly is glad to fine you. I wish you'd jes show me how to wuk this gun. I'se gwine to fight right side o' you— you heah me."

"Go back, Bob," said Crittenden, firmly.

"Silence in the ranks," roared a Lieutenant. Bob hesitated. Just then a company of the Tenth Cavalry filed down the road as they were deployed to the right. Crittenden's file of soldiers could see that the last man was a short, fat darky—evidently a recruit—and he was swinging along as jauntily as in a cake-walk. As he wheeled pompously, he dropped his gun, leaped into the air with a yell of amazed rage and pain, catching at the seat of his trousers with both hands. A bullet had gone through both buttocks.

"Gawd, Ole Cap'n, did you see dat nigger?"

A roar of laughter went down the bed of the creek.

"Go back!" repeated Crittenden, threateningly, "and stop calling me Old Captain." Bob looked after the file of coloured troops, and then at Crittenden.

"All right, Ole Cap'n; I tol' you in ole Kentuck that I gwine to fight wid the niggers ef you don't lemme fight wid you. I don't like disgracin' the family dis way, but 'tain't my fault, an' s'pose you git shot—" the slap of the flat side of a sword across Bob's back made him jump.

"What are you doing here?" thundered an angry officer. "Get into line—get into line."

"I ain't no sojer."

"Get into line," and Bob ran after the disappearing file, shaking his head helplessly.

The crash started again, and the hum of bees and the soft snap of the leaves when bullets clipped them like blows with a rattan cane, and the rattling sputter of the machine guns, and once more came that long, long wait that tries the soldier's heart, nerve, and brain.

"Why was not something done—why?"

And again rose the cry for the hospital men, and again the limp figures were brought in from the jungle, and he could see the tall doctor with the bare head helping the men who had been dressed with a first-aid bandage to the protecting bank of the creek farther up, to make room for the fresh victims. And as he stood up once, Crittenden saw him throw his hand quickly up to his temple and sink to the blood-stained sand. The assistant, who bent over him, looked up quickly and shook his head to another, who was binding a wounded leg and looking anxiously to know the fatal truth.

"I've got it," said a soldier to Crittenden's left; joyously, he said it, for the bullet had merely gone through his right shoulder. He could fight no more, he had a wound and he could wear a scar to his grave.

"So have I," said another, with a groan. And then next him there was a sudden, soft thud:

"T-h-u-p!" It was the sound of a bullet going into thick flesh, and the soldier sprang to his feet—the impulse seemed uncontrollable for the wounded to spring to their feet—and dropped with a groan—dead. Crittenden straightened him out sadly—putting his hat over his face and drawing his arms to his sides. Above, he saw with sudden nausea, buzzards circling—little cared they whether the dead were American or Spaniard, as long as there were eyes to pluck and lips to tear away, and then straightway, tragedy merged into comedy as swiftly as on a stage. Out of the woods across the way emerged a detail of negro troopers—sent to clear the woods behind of sharpshooters—and last came Bob. The detail, passing along the creek on the other bank from them, scattered, and with Bob next the creek. Bob shook his gun aloft.

"I can wuk her now!"

Another lull came, and from the thicket arose the cry of a thin, high, foreign voice:

"Americano—Americano!"

"Whut regiment you b'long to?" the voice was a negro's and was Bob's, and Grafton and Crittenden listened keenly. Bob had evidently got a sharpshooter up a tree, and caught him loading his gun.

"Tenth Cav'rly—Tenth!" was the answer. Bob laughed long and loud.

"Well, you jus the man I been lookin' fer—the fust white man I ever seed whut 'longed to a nigger regiment. Come down, honey." There was the sharp, clean crack of a Krag-Jorgensen, and a yell of savage triumph.

"That nigger's a bird," said Grafton.

Something serious was going to be done now—the intuition of it ran down the line in that mysterious fashion by which information passes down a line of waiting men. The line rose, advanced, and dropped again. Companies deployed to the left and behind—fighting their way through the chapparal as a swimmer buffets his way through choppy waves. Every man saw now that the brigade was trying to form in line of battle for a charge on that curving, smokeless flame of fire that ran to and fro around the top of the hill—blazing fiercely and steadily here and there. For half an hour the officers struggled to form the scattering men. Forward a little way; slipping from one bush and tree to another; through the thickets and bay-onet grass; now creeping; now a dash through an open spot; now flat on the stomach, until Crittenden saw a wire fence stretching ahead. Followed another wait. And then a squad of negro troopers crossed the road, going to the right, and diagonally. The bullets rained about them, and they scuttled swiftly into the brush. The hindmost one dropped; the rest kept on, unseeing; but Crittenden saw a Lieutenant—it was Sharpe, whom he had met at home and at Chickamauga—look back at the soldier, who was trying to raise himself on his elbow—while the bullets seemed literally to be mowing down the tall grass about him. Then Crittenden heard a familiar grunt behind him, and the next minute Bob's figure sprang out into the open—making for the wounded man by the sympathy of race. As he stooped, to Crittenden's horror, Bob pitched to the ground—threshing around like an animal that has received a blow on the head. Without a thought, without consciousness of his own motive or his act, Crittenden sprang to his feet and dashed for Bob. Within ten feet of the boy, his toe caught in a root and he fell headlong. As he scrambled to his feet, he saw Sharpe making for him—thinking that he had been shot down—and, as he turned, with Bob in his arms, half a dozen men, including Grafton and his own Lieutenant, were retreating back into cover—all under the same impulse and with the same motive having started for him, too. Behind a tree, Crittenden laid Bob down, still turning his head from side to side helplessly. There was a trail of blood across his temple, and, wiping it away, he saw that the bullet had merely scraped along the skull without penetrating it. In a moment, Bob groaned, opened his eyes, sat up, looked around with rolling eyes, grunted once or twice, straightened out, and reached for his gun, shaking his head.

"Gimme drink, Ole Cap'n, please, suh."

Crittenden handed him his canteen, and Bob drank and rose unsteadily to his feet.

"Dat ain't nuttin'," he said, contemptuously, feeling along the wound. "'Tain't nigh as bad as mule kick. 'Tain't nuttin', 't all." And then he almost fell.

"Go back, Bob."

163

"All right, Ole Cap'n, I reckon I'll jus' lay down heah little while," he said, stretching out behind the tree.

And Grafton reached over for Crittenden's hand. He was getting some new and startling ideas about the difference in the feeling toward the negro of the man who once owned him body and soul and of the man who freed him body and soul. And in the next few minutes he studied Crittenden as he had done before—taking in detail the long hair, lean face strongly chiselled, fearless eye, modest demeanour—marking the intellectual look of the face—it was the face of a student—a gentleman—gently born. And, there in the heat of the fight, he fell to marvelling over the nation that had such a man to send into the field as a common soldier.

Again they moved forward. Crittenden's Lieutenant dropped—wounded.

"Go on," he cried, "damn it, go on!"

Grafton helped to carry him back, stepping out into the open for him, and Crittenden saw a bullet lick up the wet earth between the correspondent's feet.

Forward again! It was a call for volunteers to advance and cut the wires. Crittenden was the first to spring to his feet, and Abe Long and Reynolds sprang after him. Forward they slipped on their bellies, and the men behind saw

one brown, knotty hand after another reach up
from the grass and clip, clip, clip through the
thickly braided wires.

Forward again! The men slipped like eels
through and under the wires, and lay in the
long grass behind. The time was come.

"FORWARD!"

Crittenden never knew before the thrill that
blast sent through him, and never in his life did
he know it again.

It was the call of America to the American,
white and black: and race and colour forgotten,
the American answered with the grit of the
Saxon, the Celt's pure love of a fight, and all the
dash of the passionate Gaul.

As Crittenden leaped to his feet, he saw Reynolds leap, too, and then there was a hissing hell
of white smoke and crackling iron at his feet—
and Reynolds disappeared.

It was a marvel afterward but, at that moment, Crittenden hardly noted that the poor
fellow was blown into a hundred fragments.
He was in the front line now. A Brigadier, with
his hat in his hand and his white hair shining in
the sun, run diagonally across in front of his
line of battle, and, with a wild cheer, the run
of death began.

God, how the bullets hissed and the shells
shrieked; and, God, how slow—slow—slow was

the run! Crittenden's legs were of lead, and leaden were the legs of the men with him—running with guns trailing the earth or caught tightly across the breast and creeping unconsciously. He saw nothing but the men in front of him, the men who were dropping behind him, and the yellow line above, and the haven at the bottom of the hill. Now and then he could see a little, dirty, blue figure leap into view on the hill and disappear. Two men only were ahead of him when he reached the foot of the hill—Sharpe and a tall Cuban close at his side with machête drawn—the one Cuban hero of that fierce charge. But he could hear laboured panting behind him, and he knew that others were coming on. God, how steep and high that hill was! He was gasping for breath now, and he was side by side with Cuban and Lieutenant—gasping, too. To right and left—faint cheers. To the right, a machine gun playing like hail on the yellow dirt. To his left a shell, bursting in front of a climbing, struggling group, and the soldiers tumbling backward and rolling ten feet down the hill. A lull in the firing—the Spaniards were running—and then the top—the top! Sharpe sprang over the trench, calling out to save the wounded. A crouching Spaniard raised his pistol, and Sharpe fell. With one leap, Crittenden reached him with the butt of his gun and, with savage exultation, he heard the skull of the Spaniard crash.

.   .   .   .

Straight in front, the Spaniards were running like rabbits through the brush. To the left, Kent was charging far around and out of sight. To the right, Rough Riders and negroes were driving Spaniards down one hill and up the next. The negroes were as wild as at a camp meeting or a voodoo dance. One big Sergeant strode along brandishing in each hand a piece of his carbine that had been shot in two by a Mauser bullet, and shouting at the top of his voice, contemptuously:

"Heah, somebody, gimme a gun! gimme a gun, I tell ye," still striding ahead and looking never behind him. "You don't know how to fight. Gimme a gun!" To the negro's left, a young Lieutenant was going up the hill with naked sword in one hand and a kodak in the other—taking pictures as he ran. A bare-headed boy, running between him and a gigantic negro trooper, toppled suddenly and fell, and another negro stopped in the charge, and, with a groan, bent over him and went no farther.

And all the time that machine gun was play-ing on the trenches like a hard rain in summer dust. Whenever a Spaniard would leap from the trench, he fell headlong. That pitiless fire kept in the trenches the Spaniards who were found there—wretched, pathetic, half-starved little creatures—and some terrible deeds were done in the lust of slaughter. One gaunt fellow thrust a clasp-knife into the buttock of a shamming Spaniard, and, when he sprang to his feet, blew the back of his head off. Some of the Riders chased the enemy over the hill and lay down in the shade. One of them pulled out of a dead Spaniard's pocket cigarettes, cigars, and a lady's slipper of white satin; with a grunt he put the slipper back. Below the trenches, two boyish prisoners sat under a tree, crying as though they were broken-hearted, and a big trooper walked up and patted them both kindly on the head.

"Don't cry, boys; it's all right—all right," he said, helplessly.

. . . .

Over at the block-house, Crittenden stopped firing suddenly, and, turning to his men, shouted:

"Get back over the hill, boys, they're going to start in again." As they ran back, a Lieutenant-Colonel met them.

"Are you in command?"

Crittenden saluted.

"No, sir," he said.

"Yes, sir," said the old Sergeant at his side. "He was. He brought these men up the hill."

"The hell he did. Where are your officers?"
The old Sergeant motioned toward the valley
below, and Crittenden opened his lips to explain,
but just then the sudden impression came to him
that some one had struck him from behind with
the butt of a musket, and he tried to wheel
around—his face amazed and wondering. Then
he dropped. He wondered, too, why he couldn't
get around, and then he wondered how it was
that he happened to be falling to the earth.
Darkness came then, and through it ran one bitter thought—he had been shot in the back. He
did think of his mother and of Judith—but it
was a fleeting vision of both, and his main
thought was a dull wonder whether there would
be anybody to explain how it was that his
wound was not in front. And then, as he felt
himself lifted, it flashed that he would at least
be found on top of the hill, and beyond the
Spaniard's trench, and he saw Blackford's face
above him. Then he was dropped heavily to
the ground again and Blackford pitched across
his body. There was one glimpse of Abe Long's
anxious face above him, another vision of Judith, and then quiet, painless darkness.

.   .   .   .

It was fiercer firing now than ever. The
Spaniards were in the second line of trenches
and were making a sortie. Under the hill sat

169

Grafton and another correspondent while the storm of bullets swept over them. Grafton was without glasses—a Mauser had furrowed the skin on the bridge of his nose, breaking his spectacle-frame so that one glass dropped on one side of his nose and the other on the other. The other man had several narrow squeaks, as he called them, and, even as they sat, a bullet cut a leaf over his head and it dropped between the pages of his note-book. He closed the book and looked up.

"Thanks," he said. "That's just what I want—I'll keep that."

"I observe," said Grafton, "that the way one of these infernal bullets sounds depends entirely on where you happen to be when you hear it. When a sharp-shooter has picked you out and is plugging at you, they are intelligent and vindictive. Coming through that bottom, they were for all the world like a lot of nasty little insects. And listen to 'em now." The other man listened. "Hear 'em as they pass over and go out of hearing. That is for all the world like the last long note of a meadow lark's song when you hear him afar off and at sunset. But I notice that simile didn't occur to me until I got under the lee of this hill." He looked around. "This hill will be famous, I suppose. Let's go up higher." They went up higher, passing a crowd of skulkers, or men in reserve—Grafton could not tell which—and as they went by a soldier said:

"Well, if I didn't have to be here, I be damned if I wouldn't like to see anybody get me here. What them fellers come fer, I can't see."

The firing was still hot when the two men got up to the danger line, and there they lay down. A wounded man lay at Grafton's elbow. Once his throat rattled and Grafton turned curiously.

"That's the death-rattle," he said to himself, and he had never heard a death-rattle before. The poor fellow's throat rattled again, and again Grafton turned.

"I never knew before," he said to himself, "that a dying man's throat rattled but once." Then it flashed on him with horror that he should have so little feeling, and he knew it at once as the curious callousness that comes quickly to toughen the heart for the sights of war. A man killed in battle was not an ordinary dead man at all—he stirred no sensation at all— no more than a dead animal. Already he had heard officers remarking calmly to one another, and apparently without feeling:

"Well, So and So was killed to-day." And he looked back to the disembarkation, when the army was simply in a hurry. Two negro troopers were drowned trying to get off on the little pier. They were fished up; a rope was tied about the neck of each, and they were lashed to the pier and left to be beaten against the wooden pillars by the waves for four hours before four comrades came and took them out and buried them. Such was the dreadful callousness that sweeps through the human heart when war begins, and he was under its influence himself, and long afterward he remembered with shame his idle and half-scientific and useless curiosity about the wounded man at his elbow. As he turned his head, the soldier gave a long, deep, peaceful sigh, as though he had gone to sleep. With pity now Grafton turned to him—and he had gone to sleep, but it was his last sleep.

"Look," said the other man. Grafton looked upward. Along the trenches, and under a hot fire, moved little Jerry Carter, with figure bent, hands clasped behind him—with the manner, for all the world, of a deacon in a country grave-yard looking for inscriptions on tombstones.

Now and then a bullet would have a hoarse sound—that meant that it had ricochetted. At intervals of three or four minutes a huge, old-fashioned projectile would labour through the air, visible all the time, and crash harmlessly into the woods. The Americans called it the "long yellow feller," and sometimes a negro trooper would turn and with a yell shoot at it as it passed over. A little way off, a squad of the Tenth Cavalry was digging a trench—close to the top of the hill. Now and then one would duck—particularly the one on the end. He had his tongue in the corner of his mouth, was twirling his pick over his shoulder like a railroad hand, and grunting with every stroke. Grafton could hear him.

"Foh Gawd (huh!) never thought (huh!) I'd git to love (huh!) a pick befoh!" Grafton broke into a laugh.

"You see the charge?"

"Part of it."

"That tall fellow with the blue handkerchief around his throat, bare-headed, long hair?"

"Well—" the other man stopped for a moment. His eye had caught sight of a figure on the ground—on the top of the trench, and with the profile of his face between him and the afterglow, and his tone changed—"there he is!"

Grafton pressed closer. "What, that the fellow?" There was the handkerchief, the head was bare, the hair long and dark. The man's eyes were closed, but he was breathing. Below them at that moment they heard the surgeon say:

"Up there." And two hospital men, with a litter, came toward them and took up the body. As they passed, Grafton recoiled.

"Good God!" It was Crittenden.

And, sitting on the edge of the trench, with Sharpe lying with his face on his arm a few feet away, and the tall Cuban outstretched beside him, and the dead Spaniards, Americans, and Cubans about them, Grafton told the story of Crittenden. And at the end the other man gave a low whistle and smote the back of one hand into the palm of the other softly.

Dusk fell quickly. The full moon rose. The stars came out, and under them, at the foot of the big mountains, a red fire burned sharply out in the mist rising over captured Caney, from which tireless Chaffee was already starting his worn-out soldiers on an all-night march by the rear and to the trenches at San Juan. And along the stormed hill-side camp-fires were glowing out where the lucky soldiers who had rations to cook were cheerily frying bacon and hardtack. Grafton moved down to watch one squad and, as he stood on the edge of the firelight, wondering at the cheery talk and joking laughter, somebody behind him said sharply:

"Watch out, there," and he turned to find himself on the edge of a grave which a detail was digging not ten yards away from the fire—digging for a dead comrade. Never had he seen a more peaceful moonlit night than the night that closed over the battlefield. It was hard for him to realize that the day had not been a terrible dream, and yet, as the moon rose, its rich light, he knew, was stealing into the guerilla-haunted jungles, stealing through guava-bush and mango-tree, down through clumps of Spanish bayonet, on stiff figures that would rise no more; on white, set faces with the peace of painless death upon them or the agony of silent torture, fought out under fierce heat and in the silence of the jungle alone.

Looking toward Caney he could even see the hill from which he had witnessed the flight of the first shell that had been the storm centre of the hurricane of death that had swept all through the white, cloudless day. It burst harmlessly—that shell—and meant no more than a signal to fire to the soldiers closing in on Caney, the Cubans lurking around a block-house at a safe artillery distance in the woods and to the impatient battery before San Juan. Retrospectively now, it meant the death-knell of brave men, the quick cry and long groaning of the wounded, the pained breathing of sick and fever-stricken, the quickened heart-beats of the waiting and anxious at home—the low sobbing of the women to whom fatal news came. It meant Cervera's gallant dash, Sampson and Schley's great victory, the fall of Santiago; freedom for Cuba, a quieter sleep for the *Maine* dead, and peace with Spain. Once more, as he rose, he looked at the dark woods, the dead-haunted jungles which the moon was draping with a more than mortal beauty, and he knew that in them, as in the long grass of the orchard-like valley below him, comrade was looking for dead comrade. And among the searchers was the faithful Bob, looking for his Old Captain, Crittenden, his honest heart nigh to bursting, for already he had found Raincrow torn with a shell and he had borne a body back to the horror-haunted little hospital under the creek bank at the Bloody Ford—a body from which the head hung over his shoulder—limp, with a bullet-hole through the neck—the body of his Young Captain, Basil.

XII

GRAFTON sat, sobered and saddened, where he was awhile. The moon swung upward white and peaceful, toward mild-eyed stars. Crickets chirped in the grass around him, and nature's low night-music started in the wood and the valley below, as though the earth had never known the hell of fire and human passion that had rocked it through that day. Was there so much difference between the creatures of the earth and the creatures of his own proud estate? Had they not both been on the same brute level that day? And, save for the wounded and the men who had comrades wounded and dead, were not the unharmed as careless, almost as indifferent as cricket and tree-toad to the tragedies of their sphere? Had there been any inner change in any man who had fought that day that was not for the worse? Would he himself get normal again, he wondered? Was there one sensitive soul who fully realized the horror of that day? If so, he would better have been at home. The one fact that stood above every thought that had come to him that day was the utter, the startling insignificance of death. Could that mean much more than a startlingly sudden lowering of the estimate put upon human life? Across the hollow behind him and from a tall palm over the Spanish trenches, rose, loud and clear, the night-song of a mocking-bird. Over there the little men in blue were toiling, toiling, toiling at their trenches; and along the crest of the hill the big men in blue were toiling, toiling, toiling at theirs. All through the night anxious eyes would be strained for Chaffee, and at dawn the slaughter would begin again. Wherever he looked, he could see with his mind's eye stark faces in the long grass of the valley and the Spanish-bayonet clumps in the woods. All day he had seen them there—dying of thirst, bleeding to death—alone. As he went down the hill, lights were moving along the creek bed. A row of muffled dead lay along the bed of the creek. Yet they were still bringing in dead and wounded—a dead officer with his will and a letter to his wife clasped in his hand. He had lived long enough to write them. Hollow-eyed surgeons were moving here and there. Up the bank of the creek, a voice rose:

"Come on, boys"—appealingly—"you're not going back on me. Come on, you cursed cowards! Good! Good! I take it back, boys. *Now* we've got 'em!"

Another voice: "Kill me, somebody—kill me. For God's sake, kill me. Won't somebody give me a pistol? God—God. . . ."

Once Grafton started into a tent. On the first cot lay a handsome boy, with a white, frank face and a bullet hole through his neck, and he recognized the dashing little fellow whom he had seen splashing through the Bloody Ford at a gallop, dropping from his horse at a barbed-wire fence, and dashing on afoot with the Rough Riders. The face bore a strong likeness to the face he had seen on the hill—of the Kentuckian, Crittenden—the Kentucky regular, as Grafton always mentally characterized him—and he wondered if the boy were not the brother of whom he had heard. The lad was still alive—but how could he live with that wound in his throat? Grafton's eyes filled with tears: it was horror— horror—all horror.

Here and there along the shadowed road lay a lifeless mule or horse or a dead man. It was curious, but a man killed in battle was not like an ordinary dead man—he was no more than he was—a lump of clay. It was more curious still that one's pity seemed less acute for man than for horse: it was the man's choice to take the risk—the horse had no choice.

Here and there by the roadside was a grave. Comrades had halted there long enough to save

a comrade from the birds of prey. Every now
and then he would meet a pack-train loaded
with ammunition and ration boxes; or a wagon
drawn by six mules and driven by a swearing,
fearless, tireless teamster. The forest was ringing with the noise of wheels, the creaking of
harness, the shouts of teamsters and the guards
with them and the officer in charge—all on the
way to the working beavers on top of the conquered hill.

Going the other way were the poor wounded,
on foot, in little groups of slowly moving twos
and threes, and in jolting, springless army
wagons—on their way of torture to more torture
in the rear. His heart bled for them. And the
way those men took their suffering! Sometimes the jolting wagons were too much for human endurance, and soldiers would pray for the
driver, when he stopped, not to start again. In
one ambulance that he overtook, a man groaned.
"Grit your teeth," said another, an old Irish
sergeant, sternly—"Grit your teeth; there's
others that's hurt worse'n you." The Sergeant
lifted his head, and a bandage showed that he
was shot through the face, and Grafton heard
not another sound. But it was the slightly hurt
—the men shot in the leg or arm—who made the
most noise. He had seen three men brought into
the hospital from San Juan. The surgeon took

the one who was groaning. He had a mere scratch on one leg. Another was dressed, and while the third sat silently on a stool, still another was attended, and another, before the surgeon turned to the man who was so patiently awaiting his turn.

"Where are you hurt?"

The man pointed to his left side.

"Through?"

"Yes, sir."

That day he had seen a soldier stagger out from the firing-line with half his face shot away and go staggering to the rear without aid. On the way he met a mounted staff officer, and he raised his hand to his hatless, bleeding forehead, in a stern salute and, without a gesture for aid, staggered on. The officer's eyes filled with tears.

"Lieutenant," said a trooper, just after the charge on the trenches, "I think I'm wounded."

"Can you get to the rear without help?"

"I think I can, sir," and he started. After twenty paces he pitched forward—dead. His wound was through the heart.

At the divisional hospital were more lights, tents, surgeons, stripped figures on the tables under the lights; rows of figures in darkness outside the tents; and rows of muffled shapes behind; the smell of anæsthetics and cleansing fluids; heavy breathing, heavy groaning, and an occasional curse on the night air.

Beyond him was a stretch of moonlit road and coming toward him was a soldier, his arm in a sling, and staggering weakly from side to side. With a start of pure gladness he saw that it was Crittenden, and he advanced with his hand outstretched.

"Are you badly hurt?"

"Oh, no," said Crittenden, pointing to his hand and arm, but not mentioning the bullet through his chest.

"Oh, but I'm glad. I thought you were gone sure when I saw you laid out on the hill."

"Oh, I am all right," he said, and his manner was as courteous as though he had been in a drawing-room; but, in spite of his nonchalance, Grafton saw him stagger when he moved off.

"I say, you oughtn't to be walking," he called. "Let me help you," but Crittenden waved him off.

"Oh, I'm all right," he repeated, and then he stopped. "Do you know where the hospital is?"

"God!" said Grafton softly, and he ran back and put his arm around the soldier—Crittenden laughing weakly:

"I missed it somehow."

"Yes, it's back here," said Grafton gently,

and he saw now that the soldier's eyes were dazed and that he breathed heavily and leaned on him, laughing and apologizing now and then with a curious shame at his weakness. As they turned from the road at the hospital entrance, Crittenden dropped to the ground.

"Thank you, but I'm afraid I'll have to rest a little while now. I'm all right now—don't bother—don't—bother. I'm all right. I feel kind o' sleepy—somehow—very kind—thank—" and he closed his eyes. A surgeon was passing and Grafton called him.

"He's all right," said the surgeon, with a swift look, adding shortly, "but he must take his turn."

Grafton passed on—sick. On along the muddy road—through more pack-trains, wagons, shouts, creakings, cursings. On through the beautiful moonlight night and through the beautiful tropical forest, under tall cocoanut and taller palm; on past the one long grave of the Rough Riders—along the battle-line of the first little fight—through the ghastly, many-coloured masses of hideous land-crabs shuffling sidewise into the cactus and shuffling on with an unearthly rustling of dead twig and fallen leaf: along the crest of the foot-hills and down to the little town of Siboney, lighted, bustling with preparation for the wounded in the tents;

bustling at the beach with the unloading of
rations, the transports moving here and there
far out on the moonlighted sea. Down there
were straggler, wounded soldier, teamster, mule-
packer, refugee Cuban, correspondent, nurse,
doctor, surgeon—the flotsam and jetsam of the
battle of the day.

.   .   .   .

The moon rose.

"Water! water! water!"

Crittenden could not move. He could see the
lights in the tents; the half-naked figures
stretched on tables; and doctors with bloody
arms about them—cutting and bandaging—one
with his hands inside a man's stomach, working
and kneading the bowels as though they were
dough. Now and then four negro troopers
would appear with something in a blanket,
would walk around the tent where there was a
long trench, and, standing at the head of this,
two would lift up their ends of the blanket and
the other two would let go, and a shapeless shape
would drop into the trench. Up and down near
by strolled two young Lieutenants, smoking cigarettes—calmly, carelessly. He could see all this,
but that was all right; that was all right! Everything was all right except that long, black shape
in the shadow near him gasping:

"Water! water! water!"

184

He could not stand that hoarse, rasping whisper much longer. His canteen he had clung to —the regular had taught him that—and he tried again to move. A thousand needles shot through him—every one, it seemed, passing through a nerve-centre and back the same path again. He heard his own teeth crunch as he had often heard the teeth of a drunken man crunch, and then he became unconscious. When he came to, the man was still muttering; but this time it was a woman's name, and Crittenden lay still. Good God!

"Judith—Judith—Judith!" each time more faintly still. There were other Judiths in the world, but the voice—he knew the voice—somewhere he had heard it. The moon was coming; it had crossed the other man's feet and was creeping up his twisted body. It would reach his face in time, and, if he could keep from fainting again, he would see.

"Water! water! water!"

Why did not some one answer? Crittenden called and called and called; but he could little more than whisper. The man would die and be thrown into that trench; or *he* might, and never know! He raised himself on one elbow again and dragged his quivering body after it; he clinched his teeth; he could hear them crunching again; he was near him now; he would not faint; and then the blood gushed from his mouth and he felt the darkness coming again, and again he heard:

"Judith—Judith!"

Then there were footsteps near him and a voice—a careless voice

"He's gone."

He felt himself caught, and turned over; a hand was put to his heart for a moment and the same voice:

"Bring in that other man; no use fooling with this one."

When the light came back to him again, he turned his head feebly. The shape was still there, but the moonlight had risen to the dead man's breast and glittered on the edge of something that was clinched in his right hand. It was a miniature, and Crittenden stared at it—unwinking—stared and stared while it slowly came into the strong, white light. It looked like the face of Judith. It wasn't, of course, but he dragged himself slowly, slowly closer. It was Judith—Judith as he had known her years ago. He must see now; he *must* see *now*, and he dragged himself on and up until his eyes bent over the dead man's face. He fell back then, and painfully edged himself away, shuddering.

"Blackford! Judith! Blackford!"

He was face to face wth the man he had

had risked their lives—men who in a fortnight had fallen from a high plane of life to the pitiful level of brutes. Only here and there was an exception. This man, Crittenden, was one. When sane, he was gentle, uncomplaining, considerate. Delirious, there was never a plaint in his voice; never a word passed his lips that his own mother might not hear; and when his lips closed, an undaunted spirit kept them firm.

"Aren't you tired?"

The nurse shook her head.

"Then you had better stay where you are; his case is pretty serious. I'll do your work for you."

The nurse nodded and smiled. She was tired and worn to death, but she sat as she was till dawn came over the sea, for the sake of the girl, whose fresh young face she saw above the sick man's heart. And she knew from the face that the other woman would have watched just that way for her.

XIII

THE thunder of big guns, Cervera's doom, and truce at the trenches. A trying week of hot sun, cool nights, tropical rains, and fevers. Then a harmless little bombardment one Sunday afternoon—that befitted the day; another week of heat and cold and wet and sickness. After that, the surrender—and the fierce little war was over.

Meantime, sick and wounded were homeward bound, and of the Crittendens Bob was the first to reach Canewood. He came in one morning, hungry and footsore, but with a swagger of importance that he had well earned.

He had left his Young Captain Basil at Old Point Comfort, he said, where the boy, not having had enough of war, had slipped aboard a transport and gone off with the Kentucky Legion for Porto Rico—the unhappy Legion that had fumed all summer at Chickamauga—and had hoisted sail for Porto Rico, without daring to look backward for fear it should be wigwagged back to land from Washington.

Was Basil well?

"Yas'm. Young Cap'n didn' min' dat little bullet right through his neck no mo'n a fly-bite. Nothin' gwine to keep dat boy back."

They had let him out of the hospital, or, rather, he had gotten out by dressing himself when his doctor was not there. An attendant tried to stop him.

"An' Young Cap'n he jes drew hisself up mighty gran' an' says: 'I'm going to join my regiment,' he says. 'It sails to-morrow.' But Ole Cap'n done killed," Bob reckoned; "killed on top of the hill where they druv the Spaniards out of the ditches whar they wus shootin' from."

Mrs. Crittenden smiled.

"No, Bob, he's coming home now," and Bob's eyes streamed. "You've been a good boy, Bob. Come here;" and she led him into the hallway and told him to wait, while she went to the door of her room and called some one.

Molly came out embarrassed, twisting a corner of her apron and putting it in her mouth while she walked forward and awkwardly shook hands.

"I think Molly has got something to say to you, Bob. You can go, Molly," she added, smiling.

The two walked toward the cabin, the negroes crowding about Bob and shaking him by the hand and asking a thousand absurd questions;

and Bob, while he was affable, was lordly as well, and one or two of Bob's possible rivals were seen to sniff, as did other young field hands, though Bob's mammy was, for the first time in her life, grinning openly with pride in her "chile," and she waved the curious away and took the two in her own cabin, reappearing presently and walking toward the kitchen.

Bob and Molly sat down on opposite sides of the fireplace, Bob triumphant at last, and Molly watching him furtively.

"I believe you has somethin' to say to me, Miss Johnson," said Bob, loftily.

"Well, I sut'nly is glad to welcome you home ag'in, Mistuh Crittenden," said Molly.

"Is you?"

Bob was quite independent now, and Molly began to weaken slightly.

"An' is dat all you got to say?"

"Ole Miss said I must tell you that I was mighty—mean—to—you—when you went—to —de wah, an' that—I'm sorry."

"Well, *is* you sorry?"

Molly was silent.

"Quit yo' foolin', gal; quit yo' foolin'."

In a moment Bob was by her side, and with his arm around her; and Molly rose to her feet with an ineffectual effort to unclasp his hands.

"Quit yo' foolin'!"

Bob's strong arms began to tighten, and the
girl in a moment turned and gave way into his
arms, and with her head on his shoulder, began
to cry. But Bob knew what sort of tears they
were, and he was as gentle as though his skin
had been as white as was his heart.

.   .   .   .

And Crittenden was coming home—Colour-
Sergeant Crittenden, who had got out of the
hospital and back to the trenches just in time to
receive flag and chevrons on the very day of
the surrender—only to fall ill of the fever and go
back to the hospital that same day. There was
Tampa once more—the great hotel, the streets,
silent and deserted, except for the occasional
officer that rode or marched through the deep dust
of the town, and the other soldiers, regulars and
volunteers, who had suffered the disappointment,
the heat, sickness, and hardship of war with little
credit from the nation at large, and no reward,
such even as a like fidelity in any path of peace
would have brought them.

Half out of his head, weak and feverish, Crittenden climbed into the dusty train and was
whirled through the dusty town, out through
dry marshes and dusty woods and dusty,
cheerless, dead-flowered fields, but with an ex-
hilaration that made his temple throb like a
woman's.

Up through the blistered, sandy, piney low-
lands; through Chickamauga again, full of
volunteers who, too, had suffered and risked
all the ills of the war without one thrill of com-
pensation; and on again, until he was once more
on the edge of the Bluegrass, with birds singing
the sun down; and again the world for him was
changed—from nervous exaltation to an air of
balm and peace; from grim hills to the rolling
sweep of low, brown slopes; from giant-poplar
to broad oak and sugar-tree; from log-cabin to
homestead of brick and stone. And so, from
mountain of Cuba and mountain of his own
land, Crittenden once more passed home. It
had been green spring for the earth when he
left, but autumn in his heart. Now autumn lay
over the earth, but in his heart was spring.

As he glanced out of the window, he could
see a great crowd about the station. A brass
band was standing in front of the station-door—
some holiday excursion was on foot, he thought.
As he stepped on the platform, a great cheer was
raised and a dozen men swept toward him,
friends, personal and political, but when they
saw him pale, thin, lean-faced, feverish, dull-
eyed, the cheers stopped and two powerful fellows took him by the arms and half carried him
to the station-door, where were waiting his
mother—and little Phyllis.

When they came out again to the carriage, the band started "Johnny Comes Marching Home Again," and Crittenden asked feebly:

"What does all this mean?"

Phyllis laughed through her tears.

"That's for you."

Crittenden's brow wrinkled in a pathetic effort to collect his thoughts; but he gave it up and looked at his mother with an unspoken question on his lips. His mother smiled merely, and Crittenden wondered why; but somehow he was not particularly curious—he was not particularly concerned about anything. In fact, he was getting weaker, and the excitement at the station was bringing on the fever again. Half the time his eyes were closed, and when he opened them on the swiftly passing autumn fields, his gaze was listless. Once he muttered several times, as though he were out of his head; and when they drove into the yard, his face was turning blue at the lips and his teeth began to chatter. Close behind came the doctor's buggy.

Crittenden climbed out slowly and slowly mounted the stiles. On the top step he sat down, looking at the old homestead and the barn and the stubble wheat-fields beyond, and at the servants coming from the quarters to welcome him, while his mother stood watching and fondly humouring him.

"Uncle Ephraim," he said to a respectful old white-haired man, "where's my buggy?"

"Right where you left it, suh."

"Well, hitch up—" Raincrow, he was about to say, and then he remembered that Raincrow was dead. "Have you got anything to drive?"

"Yessuh; we got Mr. Basil's little mare."

"Hitch her up to my buggy, then, right away. I want you to drive me."

The old darky looked puzzled, but Mrs. Crittenden, still with the idea of humouring him, nodded for him to obey, and the old man turned toward the stable.

"Yessuh—right away, suh."

"Where's Basil, mother?"

Phyllis turned her face quickly.

"He'll be here soon," said his mother, with a smile.

The doctor looked at his flushed face.

"Come on, my boy," he said, firmly. "You must get out of the sun."

Crittenden shook his head.

"Mother, have I ever done anything that you asked me not to do?"

"No, my son."

"Please don't make me begin now," he said, gently. "Is—is she at home?"

"Yes; but she is not very well. She has been ill a long while," she added, but she did not tell him that Judith had been nursing at Tampa, and that she had been sent home, stricken with fever.

The doctor had been counting his pulse, and now, with a grave look, pulled a thermometer from his pocket; but Crittenden waved him away.

"Not yet, Doctor; not yet," he said, and stopped a moment to control his voice before he went on.

"I know what's the matter better than you do. I'm going to have the fever again; but I've got something to do before I go to bed, or I'll never get up again. I have come up from Tampa just this way, and I can go on like this for two more hours; and I'm going."

The doctor started to speak, but Mrs. Crittenden shook her head at him, and Phyllis's face, too, was pleading for him.

"Mother, I'll be back in two hours, and then I'll do just what you and the doctor say; but not now."

.   .   .   .

Judith sat bare-headed on the porch with a white shawl drawn closely about her neck and about her half-bare arms. Behind her, on the floor of the porch, was, where she had thrown it, a paper in which there was a column about the home-coming of Crittenden—plain Sergeant Crittenden. And there was a long editorial comment, full of national spirit, and a plain statement to the effect that the next vacant seat in Congress was his without the asking.

The pike-gate slammed—her father was getting home from town. The buggy coming over the turf made her think what a change a few months had brought to Crittenden and to her; of the ride home with him the previous spring; and what she rarely allowed herself, she thought of the night of their parting and the warm colour came to her cheeks. He had never sent her a line, of course. The matter would never be mentioned—it couldn't be. It struck her while she was listening to the coming of the feet on the turf that they were much swifter than her father's steady-going old buggy horse. The click was different; and when the buggy, instead of turning toward the stable, came straight for the stiles, her heart quickened and she raised her head. She heard acutely the creak of the springs as some one stepped to the ground, and then, without waiting to tie his horse, stepped slowly over the stiles. Unconsciously she rose to her feet, not knowing what to think—to do. And then she saw that the man wore a slouch hat, that his coat was off, and that a huge pistol was buckled around him, and she turned for the door in alarm.

" Judith!"

The voice was weak, and she did not know it; but in a moment the light from the lamp in the hallway fell upon a bare-headed, gaunt-featured man in the uniform of a common soldier.

" Judith!"

This time the voice broke a little, and for a moment Judith stood speechless—still—unable to believe that the wreck before her was Crittenden. His face and eyes were on fire—the fire of fever—she could not know that; and he was trembling and looked hardly able to stand.

"I've come, Judith," he said. "I haven't known what to do, and I've come to tell you— to—ask——"

He was searching her face anxiously, and he stopped suddenly and passed one hand across his eyes, as though he were trying to recall something. The girl had drawn herself slowly upward until the honeysuckle above her head touched her hair, and her face, that had been so full of aching pity for him that in another moment she must have gone and put her arms about him, took on a sudden, hard quiet; and the long anguish of the summer came out suddenly in her trembling lip and the whiteness of her face.

"To ask for forgiveness," he might have said; but his instinct swerved him; and—

"For mercy, Judith," he would have said, but the look of her face stopped the words in an unheard whisper; and he stooped slowly, feeling carefully for a step, and letting himself weakly down in a way that almost unnerved her again; but he had begun to talk now, quietly and evenly, and without looking up at her.

"I'm not going to stay long. I'm not going to worry you. I'll go away in just a moment; but I had to come; I had to come. I've been a little sick, and I believe I've not quite got over the fever yet; but I couldn't go through it again without seeing you. I know that, and that's— why—I've—come. It isn't the fever. Oh, no; I'm not sick at all. I'm very well, thank you——"

He was getting incoherent, and he knew it, and stopped a moment.

"It's you, Judith——"

He stopped again, and with a painful effort went on slowly—slowly and quietly, and the girl, without a word, stood still, looking down at him.

"I—used—to—think—that—I—loved— you. I—used—to—think I was—a—man. I didn't know what love was, and I didn't know what it was to be a man. I know both now, thank God, and learning each has helped me to learn the other. If I killed all your feeling for me, I deserve the loss; but you must have known, Judith, that I was not myself that night. You did know. Your instinct told you the truth; you—knew—I loved—you—then—and that's why—that's why —you—God bless you—said—what—you—did. To think that I should ever dare to open my lips again! but I can't help it; I can't help it. I was crazy, Judith—crazy—and I am now; but it didn't go and then come back. It never went at all, as I found out, going down to Cuba—and yes, it did come back; but it was a thousand times higher and better love than it had ever been, for everything came back and I was a better man. I have seen nothing but your face all the time—nothing—nothing, all the time I've been gone; and I couldn't rest or sleep—I couldn't even die, Judith, until I had come to tell you that I never knew a man could love a woman as—I—love—you—Judith. I——"

He rose very slowly, turned, and as he passed from the light, his weakness got the better of him for the first time, because of his wounds and sickness, and his voice broke in a half sob—the sob that is so terrible to a woman's ears; and she saw him clinch his arms fiercely around his breast to stifle it.

. . . .

It was the old story that night—the story of the summer's heat and horror and suffering— heard and seen, and keenly felt in his delirium:

201

the dusty, grimy days of drill on the hot sands of Tampa; the long, long, hot wait on the transport in the harbour; the stuffy, ill-smelling breath of the hold, when the wind was wrong; the march along the coast and the grewsome life over and around him—buzzard and strange bird in the air, and crab and snail and lizard and scorpion and hairy tarantula scuttling through the tropical green rushes along the path. And the hunger and thirst and heat and dirt and rolling sweat of the last day's march and every detail of the day's fight; the stench of dead horse and dead man; the shriek of shell and rattle of musketry and yell of officer; the slow rush through the long grass, and the climb up the hill. And always, he was tramping, tramping, tramping through long, green, thick grass. Sometimes a kaleidoscope series of pictures would go jumbling through his brain, as though some imp were unrolling the scroll of his brain backward, forward, and sidewise; a whirling cloud of sand, a driving sheet of visible bullets; a hose-pipe that shot streams of melted steel; a forest of smokestacks; the flash of trailing phosphorescent foam; a clear sky, full of stars—the mountains clear and radiant through sunlit vapours; camp-fires shooting flames into the darkness, and men and guns moving past them. Through it all he could feel his legs moving and his feet tramping, tramping,

tramping through long green grass. Sometimes he was tramping toward the figure of a woman, whose face looked like Judith's; and tramp as he could, he could never get close enough through that grass to know whether it was Judith or not. But usually it was a hill that he was tramping toward, and then his foothold was good; and while he went slowly he got forward and he reached the hill, and he climbed it to a queer-looking little block-house on top, from which queer-looking little blue men were running. And now and then one would drop and not get up again. And by and by came his time to drop. Then he would begin all over again, or he would go back to the coast, which he preferred to do, in spite of his aching wound, and the long wait in the hospital and the place where poor Reynolds was tossed into the air and into fragments by a shell; in spite of the long walk back to Siboney; the graves of the Rough Riders and the scuttling land-crabs; and the heat and the smells. Then he would march back again to the trenches in his dream, as he had done in Cuba when he got out of the hospital. There was the hill up which he had charged. It looked like the abode of cave-dwellers—so burrowed was it with bomb-proofs. He could hear the shouts of welcome as his comrades, and men who had never spoken to him before, crowded about him.

How often he lived through that last proud little drama of his soldier life! There was his Captain wounded, and there was the old Sergeant—the "Governor"—with chevrons and a flag.

"You're a Sergeant, Crittenden," said the Captain.

He, Crittenden, in blood and sympathy the spirit of secession—bearer now of the Stars and Stripes! How his heart thumped, and how his head reeled when he caught the staff and looked dumbly up to the folds; and in spite of all his self-control, the tears came, as they came again and again in his delirium.

Right at that moment there was a great bustle in camp. And still holding that flag, Crittenden marched with his company up to the trenches. There was the army drawn up at parade, in a great ten-mile half-circle and facing Santiago. There were the red roofs of the town, and the batteries, which were to thunder word when the red and yellow flag of defeat went down and the victorious Stars and Stripes rose up. There were little men in straw hats and blue clothes coming from Santiago, and swinging hammocks and tethering horses in an open field, while more little men in Panama hats were advancing on the American trenches, saluting courteously. And there were American officers jumping across the trenches to meet them, and while they were shaking hands, on the very stroke of twelve, there came thunder—the thunder of two-score and one salutes. And the cheers—the cheers! From the right rose those cheers, gathering volume as they came, swinging through the centre far to the left, and swinging through the centre back again, until they broke in a wild storm against the big, green hills. A storm that ran down the foothills to the rear, was mingled with the surf at Siboney and swung by the rocking transports out to sea. Under the sea, too, it sang, along the cables, to ring on through the white corridors of the great capitol and spread like a hurricane throughout all the waiting land at home! Then he could hear bands playing—playing the "Star-Spangled Banner" —and the soldiers cheering and cheering again. Suddenly there was quiet; the bands were playing hymns—old, old hymns that the soldier had heard with bowed head at his mother's knee, or in some little old country church at home—and what hardships, privations, wounds, death of comrades had rarely done, those old hymns did now—they brought tears. Then some thoughtful soldier pulled a box of hardtack across the trenches and the little Spanish soldiers fell upon it like schoolboys and scrambled like pickaninnies for a penny.

Thus it was that day all around the shining circle of sheathed bayonets, silent carbines, and dumb cannon-mouths at the American trenches around Santiago, where the fighting was done.

And on a little knoll not far away stood Sergeant Crittenden, swaying on his feet—colour-sergeant to the folds of the ever-victorious, ever-beloved Old Glory waving over him, with a strange new wave of feeling surging through him. For then and there, Crittenden, Southerner, died straightway and through a travail of wounds, suffering, sickness, devotion, and love for that flag—Crittenden, American, was born. And just at that proud moment, he would feel once more the dizziness seize him. The world would turn dark, and again he would sink slowly.

And again, when all this was over, the sick man would go back to the long grass and tramp it once more until his legs ached and his brain swam. And when it was the hill that he could see, he was quiet and got rest for a while; and when it was the figure of Judith—he knew now that it *was* Judith—he would call aloud for her, just as he did in the hospital at Siboney. And always the tramp through the long grass would begin again—

Tramp—tramp—tramp.

He was very tired, but there was the long grass ahead of him, and he must get through it somehow.

Tramp—tramp—tramp.

.   .   .   .

XIV

AUTUMN came and the Legion was coming home—Basil was coming home. And Phyllis was for one hour haughty and unforgiving over what she called his shameful neglect and, for another, in a fever of unrest to see him. No, she was not going to meet him. She would wait for him at her own home, and he could come to her there with the honours of war on his brow and plead on bended knee to be forgiven. At least that was the picture that she sometimes surprised in her own mind, though she did not want Basil kneeling to anybody—not even to her.

The town made ready, and the spirit of welcome for the home-coming was oddly like the spirit of God-speed that had followed them six months before; only there were more smiling faces, more and madder cheers, and as many tears, but this time they were tears of joy. For many a mother and daughter who did not weep when father and brother went away, wept now, that they were coming home again. They had run the risk of fever and sickness, the real terrors of war. God knew they had done their best to get to the front, and the people knew what account they would have given of themselves had they gotten their chance at war. They had had all the hardship—the long, long hardship without the one moment of recompense that was the soldier's reward and his sole opportunity for death or glory. So the people gave them all the deserved honour that they would have given had they stormed San Juan or the stone fort at Caney. The change that even in that short time was wrought in the regiment, everybody saw; but only the old ex-Confederates and Federals on the street knew the steady, veteran-like swing of the march and felt the solid unity of form and spirit that those few months had brought to the tanned youths who marched now like soldiers indeed. And next the Colonel rode the hero of the regiment, who *had* got to Cuba, who *had* stormed the hill, and who had met a Spanish bullet face to face and come off conqueror—Basil, sitting his horse as only the Southerner, born to the saddle, can. How they cheered him, and how the gallant, generous old Colonel nodded and bowed as though to say:

"That's right; that's right. Give it to him! give it to him!"

Phyllis—her mother and Basil's mother being present—shook hands merely with Basil when

209

she saw him first at the old woodland, and Basil
blushed like a girl. They fell behind as the
older people walked toward the auditorium, and
Basil managed to get hold of her hand, but she
pulled it away rather haughtily. She was looking at him very reproachfully, a moment later,
when her eyes became suddenly fixed to the
neck of his blouse, and filled with tears. She
began to cry softly.

"Why, Phyllis."

Phyllis was giving way, and, thereupon, with
her own mother and Basil's mother looking on,
and to Basil's blushing consternation, she darted
for his neck-band and kissed him on the throat.
The throat flushed, and in the flush a tiny white
spot showed—the mouth of a tiny wound where
a Mauser bullet had hissed straight through.

Then the old auditorium again, and Crittenden, who had welcomed the Legion to camp at
Ashland, was out of bed, against the doctor's
advice, to welcome it to home and fireside. And
when he faced the crowd—if they cheered Basil,
what did they do now? He was startled by the
roar that broke against the roof. As he stood
there, still pale, erect, modest, two pairs of eyes
saw what no other eyes saw, two minds were
thinking what none others were—the mother
and Judith Page. Others saw him as the soldier, the generous brother, the returned hero.

These two looked deeper and saw the new man who had been forged from dross by the fire of battle and fever and the fire of love. There was much humility in the face, a new fire in the eyes, a nobler bearing—and his bearing had always been proud—a nobler sincerity, a nobler purpose.

He spoke not a word of himself—not a word of the sickness through which he had passed. It was of the long patience and the patriotism of the American soldier, the hardship of camp life, the body-wearing travail of the march in tropical heat. And then he paid his tribute to the regular. There was no danger of the volunteer failing to get credit for what he had done, but the regular—there was no one to speak for him in camp, on the transports, on the march, in tropical heat, and on the battle-field. He had seen the regular hungry, wet, sick, but fighting still; and he had seen him wounded, dying, dead, and never had he known anything but perfect kindness from one to the other; perfect courtesy to outsider; perfect devotion to officer, and never a word of complaint—never one word of complaint.

"Sometimes I think that the regular who has gone will not open his lips if the God of Battles tells him that not yet has he earned eternal peace."

As for the war itself, it had placed the nation high among the seats of the Mighty. It had increased our national pride, through unity, a thousand fold. It would show to the world and to ourselves that the heroic mould in which the sires of the nation were cast is still casting the sons of to-day; that we need not fear degeneracy nor dissolution for another hundred years—smiling as he said this, as though the dreams of Greece and Rome were to become realities here. It had put to rest for a time the troublous social problems of the day; it had brought together every social element in our national life—coal-heaver and millionaire, student and cowboy, plain man and gentleman, regular and volunteer —had brought them face to face and taught each for the other tolerance, understanding, sympathy, high regard; and had wheeled all into a solid front against a common foe. It had thus not only brought shoulder to shoulder the brothers of the North and South, but those brothers shoulder to shoulder with our brothers across the sea. In the interest of humanity, it had freed twelve million people of an alien race and another land, and it had given us a better hope for the alien race in our own.

And who knew but that, up where France's great statue stood at the wide-thrown portals of the Great City of the land, it had not given to

the mighty torch that nightly streams the light
of Liberty across the waters from the New World
to the Old—who knew that it had not given to
that light a steady, ever-onward-reaching glow
that some day should illumine the earth?

.   .   .   .

The Cuban fever does not loosen its clutch
easily.

Crittenden went to bed that day and lay there
delirious and in serious danger for more than
a fortnight. But at the end a reward came for
all the ills of his past and all that could ever
come.

His long fight was over, and that afternoon
he lay by his window, which was open to the
rich, autumn sunlight that sifted through the
woods and over the pasture till it lay in golden
sheens across the fence and the yard and rested
on his window-sill, rich enough almost to grasp
with his hand, should he reach out for it. There
was a little colour in his face—he had eaten one
good meal that day, and his long fight with the
fever was won. He did not know that in his
delirium he had spoken of Judith—Judith—
Judith—and this day and that had given out
fragments from which his mother could piece
out the story of his love; that, at the crisis, when
his mother was about to go to the girl, Judith
had come of her own accord to his bedside. He

did not know her, but he grew quiet at once when the girl put her hand on his forehead.

Now Crittenden was looking out on the sward, green with the curious autumn-spring that comes in that Bluegrass land: a second spring that came every year to nature, and was coming this year to him. And in his mood for field and sky was the old, dreamy mistiness of pure delight—spiritual—that he had not known for many years. It was the spirit of his youth come back—that distant youth when the world was without a shadow; when his own soul had no tarnish of evil; when passion was unconscious and pure; when his boyish reverence was the only feeling he knew toward every woman. And lying thus, as the sun sank and the shadows stole slowly across the warm bands of sunlight, and the meadow-lark called good-night from the meadows, whence the cows were coming homeward and the sheep were still browsing—out of the quiet and peace and stillness and purity and sweetness of it all came his last vision—the vision of a boy with a fresh, open face and no shadow across the mirror of his clear eyes. It looked like Basil, but it was "the little brother" of himself coming back at last—coming with a glad, welcoming smile. The little man was running swiftly across the fields toward him. He had floated lightly over the fence, and was making straight across the yard for his window; and there he rose and floated in, and with a boy's trustfulness put his small, chubby hand in the big brother's, and Crittenden felt the little fellow's cheek close to his as he slept on, his lashes wet with tears.

The mother opened the door; a tall figure slipped gently in; the door was closed softly after it again, and Judith was alone; for Crittenden still lay with his eyes closed, and the girl's face whitened with pity and flamed slowly as she slowly slipped forward and stood looking down at him. As she knelt down beside him, something that she held in her hand clanked softly against the bed and Crittenden opened his eyes.

"Mother!"

There was no answer. Judith had buried her face in her hands. A sob reached his ears and he turned quickly.

"Judith," he said; "Judith," he repeated, with a quick breath. "Why, my God, you! Why—you—you've come to see me! you, after all—you!"

He raised himself slowly, and as he bent over her, he saw his father's sword, caught tightly in her white hands—the old sword that was between him and Basil to win and wear— and he knew the meaning of it all, and he had to steady himself to keep back his own tears.

" Judith!"

His voice choked; he could get no further, and he folded his arms about her head and buried his face in her hair.

XV

THE gray walls of Indian summer tumbled at the horizon and let the glory of many fires shine out among the leaves. Once or twice the breath of winter smote the earth white at dawn. Christmas was coming, and God was good that Christmas.

Peace came to Crittenden during the long, dream-like days—and happiness; and high resolve had deepened.

Day by day, Judith opened to him some new phase of loveliness, and he wondered how he could have ever thought that he knew her; that he loved her, as he loved her now. He had given her the locket and had told her the story of that night at the hospital. She had shown no surprise, and but very little emotion; moreover, she was silent. And Crittenden, too, was silent, and, as always, asked no questions. It was her secret; she did not wish him to know, and his trust was unfaltering. Besides, he had his secrets as well. He meant to tell her all some day, and she meant to tell him; but the hours we re so full of sweet companionship that both forbore to throw the semblance of a shadow on the sunny days they spent together.

It was at the stiles one night that Judith handed Crittenden back the locket that had come from the stiffened hand of the Rough Rider, Blackford, along with a letter, stained, soiled, unstamped, addressed to herself, marked on the envelope "Soldier's letter," and counter-signed by his Captain.

"I heard him say at Chickamauga that he was from Kentucky," ran the letter, "and that his name was Crittenden. I saw your name on a piece of paper that blew out of his tent one day. I guessed what was between you two, and I asked him to be my 'bunkie;' but as you never told him my name, I never told him who I was. I went with the Rough Riders, but we have been camped near each other. To-morrow comes the big fight. Our regiments will doubtless advance together. I shall watch out for him as long as I am alive. I shall be shot. It is no premonition —no fear, no belief. I know it. I still have the locket you gave me. If I could, I would give it to him; but he would know who I am, and it seems your wish that he should not know. I should like to see you once more, but I should not like you to see me. I am too much changed; I can see it in my own face. Good-night. Good-by."

There was no name signed. The initials were J. P., and Crittenden looked up inquiringly.

"His name was not Blackford; it was Page— Jack Page. He was my cousin," she went on, gently. "That is why I never told you. It all happened while you were at college. While you were here, he was usually out West; and people thought we were merely cousins, and that I was weaning him from his unhappy ways. I was young and foolish, but I had—you know the rest."

The tears gathered in her eyes.

"God pity him!"

Crittenden turned from her and walked to and fro, and Judith rose and walked up to him, looking him in the eyes.

"No, dear," she said; "I am sorry for him now—sorry, so sorry! I wish I could have helped him more. That is all. It has all gone— long ago. It never was. I did not know until I left you here at the stiles that night."

Crittenden looked inquiringly into her eyes before he stooped to kiss her. She answered his look.

"Yes," she said simply; "when I sent him away."

Crittenden's conscience smote him sharply. What right had he to ask such a question—even with a look?

"Come, dear," he said; "I want to tell you all—now."

But Judith stopped him with a gesture.

"Is there anything that may cross your life hereafter—or mine?"

"No, thank God; no!"

Judith put her finger on his lips.

"I don't want to know."

.   .   .   .

And God was good that Christmas.

The day was snapping cold, and just a fortnight before Christmas eve. There had been a heavy storm of wind and sleet the night before, and the negroes of Canewood, headed by Bob and Uncle Ephraim, were searching the woods for the biggest fallen oak they could find. The frozen grass was strewn with wrenched limbs, and here and there was an ash or a sugar-tree splintered and prostrate, but wily Uncle Ephraim was looking for a yule-log that would burn slowly and burn long; for as long as the log burned, just that long lasted the holiday of every darky on the place. So the search was careful, and lasted till a yell rose from Bob under a cliff by the side of the creek—a yell of triumph that sent the negroes in a rush toward him. Bob stood on the torn and twisted roots of a great oak that wind and ice had tugged from its creek-washed roots and stretched parallel

with the water—every tooth showing delight in
his find. With the cries and laughter of children, two boys sprang upon the tree with axes,
but Bob waved them back.

"Go back an' git dat cross-cut saw!" he
said.

Bob, as ex-warrior, took precedence even of
his elders now.

"Fool niggers don't seem to know dar'll
be mo' wood to burn if we don't waste de
chips!"

The wisdom of this was clear, and, in a few
minutes, the long-toothed saw was singing
through the tough bark of the old monarch—a
darky at each end of it, the tip of his tongue in
the corner of his mouth, the muscles of each
powerful arm playing like cords of elastic steel
under its black skin—the sawyers, each time
with a mighty grunt, drew the shining, whistling
blade to and fro to the handle. Presently they
began to sing—improvising:

> Pull him t'roo! (grunt)
> Yes, man.
> Pull him t'roo—huh!
> Saw him to de heart.
>
> .   .   .   .   .   .
>
> Gwine to have Christmas.
> Yes, man!
> Gwine to have Christmas.
> Yes, man!

Gwine to have Christmas
   Long as he can bu'n.

.   .   .   .   .   .

Burn long, log!
   Yes, log!
Burn long, log!
   Yes, log,
Heah me, log, burn long!

Gib dis nigger Christmas.
   Yes, Lawd, long Christmas!
Gib dis nigger Christmas.
   O log, burn long!

And the saw sang with them in perfect time,
spitting out the black, moist dust joyously—
sang with them and without a breath for rest;
for as two pair of arms tired, another fresh pair
of sinewy hands grasped the handles. In an
hour the whistle of the saw began to rise in key
higher and higher, and as the men slowed up
carefully, it gave a little high squeak of triumph,
and with a "kerchunk" dropped to the ground.
With more cries and laughter, two men rushed
for fence-rails to be used as levers.

There was a chorus now:

Soak him in de water,
   Up, now!
Soak him in de water,
   Up, now!
O Lawd, soak long!

There was a tightening of big, black biceps, a swelling of powerful thighs, a straightening of mighty backs; the severed heart creaked and groaned, rose slightly, turned and rolled with a great splash into the black, winter water. Another delighted chorus:

"Dyar now!"

"Hol' on," said Bob; and he drove a spike into the end of the log, tied one end of a rope to the spike, and the other to a pliant young hickory, talking meanwhile:

"Gwine to rain, an' maybe ole Mister Log try to slip away like a thief in de dark. Don't git away from Bob; no suh. You be heah now Christmas eve—sho'!"

"Gord!" said a little negro with bandy legs. "Soak dat log till Christmas an' I reckon he'll burn mo'n two weeks."

God was good that Christmas—good to the nation, for He brought to it victory and peace, and made it one and indivisible in feeling, as it already was in fact; good to the State, for it had sprung loyally to the defence of the country, and had won all the honour that was in the effort to be won, and man nor soldier can do more; good to the mother, for the whole land rang with praises of her sons, and her own people swore that to one should be given once more the seat of his fathers in the capitol; but best to her when the bishop came to ordain, and, on his knees at the chancel and waiting for the good old man's hands, was the best beloved of her children and her first-born—Clay Crittenden. To her a divine purpose seemed apparent, to bring her back the best of the old past and all she prayed for the future.

As Christmas day drew near, gray clouds marshalled and loosed white messengers of peace and good-will to the frozen earth until the land was robed in a thick, soft, shining mantle of pure white—the first spiritualization of the earth for the birth of spring. It was the mother's wish that her two sons should marry on the same day and on that day, and Judith and Phyllis yielded. So early that afternoon, she saw together Judith, as pure and radiant as a snow-hung willow in the sunshine, and her son, with the light in his face for which she had prayed so many years—saw them standing together and clasp hands forever. They took a short wedding trip, and that straight across the crystal fields, where little Phyllis stood with Basil in uniform—straight and tall and with new lines, too, but deepened merely, about his handsome mouth and chin—waiting to have their lives made one. And, meanwhile, Bob and Molly too were making ready; for if there be a better hot-bed of sentiment than the mood of man and woman when the man is going to war,

it is the mood of man and woman when the man
has come home from war; and with cries and
grunts and great laughter and singing, the negroes were pulling the yule-log from its long
bath and across the snowy fields; and when, at
dusk, the mother brought her two sons and her
two daughters and the Pages and Stantons to
her own roof, the big log, hidden by sticks of
pine and hickory, was sputtering Christmas
cheer with a blaze and crackle that warmed body
and heart and home. That night the friends
came from afar and near; and that night Bob,
the faithful, valiant Bob, in a dress-suit that was
his own and new, and Mrs. Crittenden's own
gift, led the saucy Molly, robed as no other
dusky bride at Canewood was ever arrayed, into
the dining-room, while the servants crowded the
doors and hallway and the white folk climbed
the stairs to give them room. And after a few
solemn moments, Bob caught the girl in his
arms and smacked her lips loudly:

"Now, gal, I reckon I got yer!" he cried;
and whites and blacks broke into jolly laughter,
and the music of fiddles rose in the kitchen,
where there was a feast for Bob's and Molly's
friends. Rose, too, the music of fiddles under
the stairway in the hall, and Mrs. Crittenden
and Judge Page, and Crittenden and Mrs.
Stanton, and Judith and Basil, and none other

than Grafton and radiant little Phyllis led the way for the opening quadrille. It was an old-fashioned Christmas the mother wanted, and an old-fashioned Christmas, with the dance and merriment and the graces of the old days, that the mother had. Over the portrait of the eldest Crittenden, who slept in Cuba, hung the flag of the single star that would never bend its colours again to Spain. Above the blazing log and over the fine, strong face of the brave father, who had fought to dissolve the Union, hung the Stars and Bars—proudly. And over the brave brother, who looked down from the north wall, hung proudly the Stars and Stripes for which he had given his young life.

Then came toasts after the good old fashion—graceful toasts—to the hostess and the brides, to the American soldier, regular and volunteer. And at the end, Crittenden, regular, raised his glass and there was a hush.

It was good, he said, to go back to the past; good to revive and hold fast to the ideals that time had proven best for humanity; good to go back to the earth, like the Titans, for fresh strength; good for the man, the State, the nation. And it was best for the man to go back to the ideals that had dawned at his mother's knee; for there was the fountain-head of the nation's faith in its God, man's faith in his nation—man's faith in his fellow and faith in himself. And he drank to one who represented his own early ideals better than he should ever realize them for himself. Then he raised his glass, smiling, but deeply moved:

"My little brother."

He turned to Basil when he spoke and back again to Judith, who, of all present, knew all that he meant, and he saw her eyes shine with the sudden light of tears.

At last came the creak of wheels on the snow outside, the cries of servants, the good-bys and good-wishes and congratulations from one and all to one and all; the mother's kiss to Basil and Phyllis, who were under their mother's wing; the last calls from the doorway; the light of lanterns across the fields; the slam of the pike-gate —and, over the earth, white silence. The mother kissed Judith and kissed her son.

"My children!"

Then, as was her custom always, she said simply:

"Be sure to bolt the front door, my son."

And, as he had done for years, Crittenden slipped the fastenings of the big hall-door, paused a moment, and looked out. Around the corner of the still house swept the sounds of merriment from the quarters. The moon had risen on the snowy fields and white-cowled trees and draped hedges and on the slender white shaft under the bent willow over his father's and his uncle's grave—the brothers who had fought face to face and were sleeping side by side in peace, each the blameless gentleman who had reverenced his conscience as his king, and, without regret for his way on earth, had set his foot, without fear, on the long way into the hereafter. For one moment his mind swept back over the short, fierce struggle of the summer.

As they had done, so he had tried to do; and as they had lived, so he, with God's help, would live henceforth to the end. For a moment he thought of the flag hanging motionless in the dim drawing-room behind him—the flag of the great land that was stretching out its powerful hand to the weak and oppressed of the earth. And then with a last look to the willow and the shaft beneath, his lips moved noiselessly:

"They will sleep better to-night."

Judith was standing in the drawing-room on his hearth, looking into his fire and dreaming. Ah, God, to think that it should come to pass at last!

He entered so softly that she did not hear him. There was no sound but the drowsy tick of the great clock in the hall and the low song of the fire.

"Sweetheart!"

She looked up quickly, the dream gone from her face, and in its place the light of love and perfect trust, and she stood still, her arms hanging at her sides—waiting.

"Sweetheart!"

God was good that Christmas.

THE END